PRAISE FOR

"Heighton is an experienced adventurer in literary form . . . A sense of boldness and risk-taking infuses [his work]." — *New York Times Book Review*

"Deservedly won a Governor General's Award . . . Richly rewarding on repeated reading . . . The poems are by turns angry, elegiac, or simply intoxicated with wordplay and the intricacy of assonance." — John Doyle, *Globe and Mail*, on *The Waking Comes Late*

"A supremely cohesive and coherent performance . . . The poems speak to (or with) readers, a rare anomaly in these times . . . Heighton works (and plays) with words in wondrous ways few contemporary poets even dream of attempting, let alone conquering." — Judith Fitzgerald, *Globe and Mail*, on *Patient Frame*

"Arrestingly beautiful and never banal . . . Authoritative and intoxicating . . . Stylistically and formally various . . . [Heighton] is a singer in an age-old tradition pursuing his serious craft." — *Journal of Canadian Poetry* on *The Address Book*

"Simply the most exciting book of poetry published this year." — *Globe and Mail* on *The Ecstasy of Skeptics*

"A sensitively conceived collection strong in poetic form, lyricism and emotion . . . A virtuoso performance." — Governor General's Literary Award Jury Citation on *The Ecstasy of Skeptics*

"Introduces a major new voice . . . Written in a style that is both elegant and free-flowing." — *Montreal Gazette* on *Foreign Ghosts*

"A forgotten ur-text to so much of what Canadian poetry has become in the intervening quarter century since its publication . . . It would take another twenty-five years for Canadian poetry to catch up to the ambitious synthesis of sonic lushness and thematic unity that Heighton achieved in his first book."
— Michael Lista, *National Post*, on the re-issued *Stalin's Carnival*

SELECTED POEMS 1983–2020

STEVEN HEIGHTON

EDITED BY KAREN SOLIE

ANANSI

Published in Canada in 2021 and the USA in 2021 by House of Anansi Press Inc.
www.houseofanansi.com

House of Anansi Press and the author are grateful to publisher Aimée Parent Dunn for permission to reprint poems from *Stalin's Carnival*. The first edition was published by Quarry Press (Kingston, ON) in 1989; the second edition was published by Palimpsest Press (Kingsville, ON) in 2013.

House of Anansi Press is committed to protecting our natural environment. This book is made of material from well-managed FSC®-certified forests and other controlled sources.

House of Anansi Press is a Global Certified Accessible™ (GCA by Benetech) publisher. The ebook version of this book meets stringent accessibility standards and is available to students and readers with print disabilities.

25 24 23 22 21   1 2 3 4 5

Library and Archives Canada Cataloguing in Publication

Title: Selected poems 1983–2020 / Steven Heighton.
Other titles: Poems. Selections (2021)
Names: Heighton, Steven, author.
Identifiers: Canadiana (print) 2020034272X | Canadiana (ebook) 20200342754 |
ISBN 9781487007379 (softcover) | ISBN 9781487007386 (EPUB) |
ISBN 9781487009212 (Kindle)
Classification: LCC PS8565.E451 A6 2021 | DDC C811/.54—dc23

Cover design: Alysia Shewchuk
Text design and typesetting: Laura Brady

House of Anansi Press respectfully acknowledges that the land on which we operate is the Traditional Territory of many Nations, including the Anishinabeg, the Wendat, and the Haudenosaunee. It is also the Treaty Lands of the Mississaugas of the Credit.

 Canada Council   Conseil des Arts
for the Arts   du Canada
 ONTARIO ARTS COUNCIL
CONSEIL DES ARTS DE L'ONTARIO

We acknowledge for their financial support of our publishing program the Canada Council for the Arts, the Ontario Arts Council, and the Government of Canada.

Printed and bound in Canada

Flight Path of the Emperor

This book, like my first, is dedicated to John McEwen Heighton, who long ago walked me to the trailhead and gave me a compass, but refused to burden me with directions or a map.

CONTENTS

FOREIGN GHOSTS (1990)

THE ECSTASY OF SKEPTICS (1994)

THE ADDRESS BOOK (2004)

PATIENT FRAME (2010)

THE WAKING COMES LATE (2016)

NEW POEMS

Jun 30

Until recently, if you'd bothered to ask me how I thought my poetry had changed over the past third of a century or so, I might have replied that two sources of inspiration have increasingly contributed to the work: dreams (usually in the form of lines overheard, so to speak, in sleep and transcribed on waking) and the practice of translating other poets.

But after reading through my six collections, then weighing in on Karen Solie's triage as she selected the poems for this book, I see that my reply would have been wrong. Dream materials and the act of translation have nourished the work from the start. My first published poem, "Nightmare," is a transcription of a dream — or, if I remember right, a kind of translation of imagery into verbal form. Another early poem, "Restless," features a refrain translated (by means of a century-old, twenty-five-pound dictionary) from an Old Norse lyric I've never been able to find since. And the suite of poems at the centre of my first book, *Stalin's Carnival*, consists of pseudo-translations I wrote after first roughly translating an actual early poem by Josef Djugashvili (the young man who later translated himself into Josef Stalin).

I wrote my second book, *Foreign Ghosts*, while backpacking through Asia and then teaching English in Japan, where I practiced a kind of diseased frugality in hopes of saving enough money to write full-time on my return. I also taught myself some Japanese, and I see now that translation and mistranslation, both verbal and cultural, are the tectonic forces underlying that collection.

In the four books that follow, dream poems appear with increasing frequency, along with free translations — approximations, I started calling them — of poems modern and ancient, renowned and obscure. In *The Address Book* and *Patient Frame* I sequestered these approximations at the end, but in my most recent collection, *The Waking Comes Late*, I integrated them with my own work. While this approach might seem to propose an equality between lines of my own and, say, classic cadences by Sappho, the interleaving really just reflects how the material in any one book emerges from a single creative period, a unified process of reading, writing, and revising. I work on approximations concurrently with my own poems, so the two forms are always in dialogue on my desk — my engagement with a poem by Georg Trakl, say, inspiring a poem of my own, which then suggests ways to improve the translation. I regret there wasn't room to include more approximations here, especially my version of Rimbaud's hundred-line *Le Bateau ivre,* on which I worked for two years, loving every arduous minute.

Discerning patterns in your own work, even if it takes decades, is still easier than trying to explain them. But I will say this much. From the start, the part of my mind that conceives real poems (as opposed to the ego that forces fakes) seems to have worked to subvert my tendency to overthink and over-explain the world. It has recruited me into the role of stenographer to my nightmind; it has nudged me toward difficult, hence usefully estranging, languages and the act of translation — which, like dreams, demotes the bossy, noisy ego, since translators must submit and apprentice themselves to the source text and labour in service to it.

And then music. That's the other thread that holds these poems together, I hope, across decades. In my teens and early twenties I wrote songs, then began to focus on poetry — though the poetry always seemed an extension of the songwriting impulse, and perhaps by not singing the words, or accompanying them on guitar, I placed a healthy pressure on them to make their own music.

These last few years I've returned to music. Maybe I sensed it was time to take my poetry back to its roots — back to where poetry itself began, long ago — in song. Or maybe, as John Prine put it, "Your heart gets bored with your mind and it changes you." Sing the words instead of write them and it's harder to overthink them — so at last nothing stands between your heart and your hearer. If I'm lucky and poems, too, keep coming, I'll hope this arc of return infuses the work with a deeper music, a fuller openness.

I'm grateful to my poetry publisher, House of Anansi, for bringing out this selected poems volume. Thank you especially to Karen Solie; to Anansi's poetry editor, Kevin Connolly; and to its managing editor, Maria Golikova.

— STEVEN HEIGHTON, Kingston, November 2020

SELECTED POEMS 1983–2020

STALIN'S CARNIVAL

(1989, re-issued 2013)

Early Poems, 1983–1986

ENDURANCE

At the crack she pounced
hours over the grip of pool, she split
the skin and sheered like a seawind back

to breast the surface, ripple with fluid
motion toward a standing wall. She coiled,
sprang, and her back broke

water, fin-slick, arched again and drove.
Someday the water's skin will not give,
its flesh will stiffen around her, gathering

strands of her hair and strength, and spirit them
down like a moon through the tidal pools.
Her crawl will slacken but discover in rest

the power of sea-beds, mussels, coral
that forge in the rhythms of sleep a pearl
of flesh. See her flail with brief endurance—

when the race ends, there is still this.

SAILING, GULF ISLANDS

Let me remember

my father. How he
swooped like a diving gull under the swung
boom and we ran
steady, before the winds in early evening
failed.
Sail's flap
and sweet strain in a fathering gust,
how I gripped whiteknuckled and leaned

years back

till scud and the speed-
warm sea slapped
in my hair, my father

there with the rudder kept the stone-
fragrant shores to port, to bright star-
board a blue vaulting of shoalcold spaces
banked with windwall and towering cloud . . .

I remember now

like a conscious poet
that fugitive harmony,
child's sphere,
half my brain asleep, the other teeming, almost
curled in the cool sail's belly
till the wind died.
Lies,
I dredge them up again, again and run
aground on the steaming seacoasts I recall,

　　　　　　　　　　　　　　　　or do I invent
those graveyards of the dreamed Pacific?

　　　　　　　　　　　Face rimed with salt I am still
that child leaning back,
a craft standing at anchor
in the sounds and green havens of fiction.

A PERISHABLE ART

I found my mother's footprints in the snow
still fresh, she'd passed this way only moments before.
Her tracks climbed and crossed the treeless hills at the skyline.
Her heels were halfmoon gouges in the white crust, glowing.

The prints held no warmth. Their shapes already changing.
Surprising how directly she had managed
to shear through that wandering terrain, as if
something unusual in the windempty range

of hills had captured her eye and drawn her on
with a purpose. And in fact all the signs there were
pointed to this — the long intervals between prints
suggesting haste, their unfaltering

evenness betraying a certain intensity, a certain
determination. I followed them some distance, saw nothing
but blue sky white hills and shadows between hills
and the prints themselves receding, as if by plan

clean as a survey trail or concession road . . .
Before dark it grew windy. Powder snow
rippled like gauze curtains between hills, and quickly
filled in footprints — mine behind me
                                    and my mother's before.

RESTLESS

Man to the hills, woman to the shore
— Gaelic proverb quoted by Seamus Heaney in *Wintering Out*

Pensiones line Corfu Bay
but I followed the coast, then went inland.
The one form on a dry black road, I

cannot sleep on the banks of the sea.

And on Skye, when an overgrown cart-trail
ended in a cove by a ruined pier, I climbed
a gullswept cliff and slept in the hills, because I

cannot sleep on the banks of the sea.

Lay last on the brine-bitter
stones of Galway, my feet in flotsam
drying between tides, but woke soon
restless, thirsty and cold,
one form unlulled by the ocean, I

cannot sleep on the banks of the sea.

HIGH JUMP

Four strides the legs compass, close,
burst gravity's shell and vault

as sunrise at the pole bends
back, sickles the sun-

sleek arc of dolphin, diver, gull,
his skull at noon and hovering. There

the body contends with higher things —
sharp light, thinning air; the eclipse

and setting of records; a fixed
orbit he believes he frames. At his height

he wavers, reels like a lover and prays
his lunging survives him

in a perfect act; feels time
tug at his second hand

as the earth draws breath, pole
and body into ground. Hear it:

a hissing of wind in the high
arena, and his spikes

rattle, raised like knuckles at the sky.

INUKSUK

We found him first in early spring
standing alone under the eye-
teeth of an inland range

A stunted form, bewildered
by the longer shadows of peaks, he cast
an image, dim
as a minute hand
and circled hours on snow.

We passed him again in August
on a wide plain rimmed
with brilliant hills,
worn smaller now, the body
rimed with lichen, limbs
blunt gestures of shale —

quarried once in the low hills
he had been changed
the tundra conspiring around him

to this dune of rubble
like sand in an hourglass —
we tracked his gaze to the lowland.

And September, with the new hail
cobbling the seacoast,
we found him at last, eroded
grey as beached bone —

a dwarf aging among barrows he
saw us push from shore
leaving as his makers had

His face could not even accuse
but bore betrayal
with the amazed endurance
of a likeness, unfinished,
or a forgotten god.

Inuksuit: *Stone cairns, some of them vaguely human in form, erected by the Inuit as
navigational markers, among other purposes. "Inuksuk" is the singular form.*

THE MACHINE GUNNER

I saw them. They came like ghosts out of ground-
mist, moving
over ruined earth in waves, running,

no, walking, shoulder to shoulder
like a belt of bullets or like
men: tinned meat lined on a conveyor belt as the sun

exploded in thin shafts on metal
buckles, bayonets, the nodding
spires of helmets. I heard faint battle cries

and whistles, piercing through the shriek
of fire and iron falling, the slurred
cadence of big guns. As they funnelled

like a file of mourners into gaps
in the barbed wire, I made quick
calculations and slipped the safety catch.

But held my fire. Alongside me
the boys in the trenches worried them with
rifles, pistols, hand grenades

but they came on, larger now, their faces
almost resolving out of hazed, hot
distance, their ranks at close quarters amazing

with dumb courage, numb step, a sound of drugged
choking in gas and green mud, steaming . . .
Who were these men. I saw them penitent,

sagging to knees. I saw their dishevelled
dying. And when finally they broke
into a run it came to me

what they had always been, how I'd always,
really, seen them: boys
rushing toward us with arms

outstretched, hands clenched as if in urgent
prayer, welcome, or a reunion
quite unexpected. Yes. And more than this

like children, chased by something behind the lines
and hurrying to us
for rescue . . .

I spat and swung the gun around. Fired,
felt the metal pulse
and laid them three deep in the wire.

THE BURNED OUT SLOPE

Skull-shapes in deadfall, sockets in rotting pine
reprove our slow approach
with anthropomorphic eyes.

Where whitened horns record the sun's transits
charred trunks tapered by years
fill an east wind with invisible spores,
feeding saxifrage and lichen,
fuelling cycles of unchanging flux . . .

And I am here
after trying so long to exile
the imperious eye
to listen with ear primed
at the rock's heart
for the swarming of molecules
the sullen locutions of an empty land
— lake wind river stone
fire that clambered up these slopes
like cloudshadow over a mountainside
with or without us making forests fall
and carving symbols of them.

Elk Lake

INVENTION

Tell me the word, mother, if you know now,
The word known to all men.

Because she had watched seedlings grow
too often through double-panes of her storm
window;

because pineneedles, honed by sunlight,
brushed the screen softly but
would not penetrate its mesh

she invented a garden
indoors, under a bay window,
filling it with herbs.

           Still, it was the word
for each plant she thought of first
on waking: tarragon,
ivy and lavender, sorrel, coriander,
rue. The double names recited themselves
in her halfsleep: nightshade,
rattlegrass and goldenrod,
heart's ease.
          And when she walked up the sunpaved hall
to her garden, the lambent blossoms,
the slight wavering stalks that might have belonged
in a bird's delicate skeleton
filled the room with a forest
of syllables, green
and speechless as a bird's call —

tangible as first metaphor —
                Eden.

NIGHTMARE

I will be standing
on the verge of a plain
by a highway no one else has taken

Flat dance of the skyline
skin burned by a treeless sun
somewhere the roar of an ocean

                                     or a silver car

that slows and stops
a door that swings

and I must choose
on the verge of the plain —
and though it is hard to see

through the layering dust
I believe I hoist my bag and
pull it after me

into that car,

From *Ashes on the Earth: Selected Works of Josef Stalin*

Only in Russia is poetry respected; it gets people killed. Is there anywhere else where poetry is so common a motive for murder?

— Osip Mandelstam

1. TO THE MOON

> *In his early poems Stalin makes no effort to conceal his emotions, and he shows*
> *clearly that he was capable of genuine religious feeling and possessed a romantic*
> *attachment to the oppressed, following a centuries-old poetic tradition. Already*
> *there is evidence of a small but real poetic talent.*
>
> — Robert Payne, *The Rise and Fall of Stalin*

Move on, inexhaustible one —
Never bowing your round, scarved head,
Scatter the misty clouds,
Great is the providence of the Almighty.
Gaze gently upon the busy world
That lies outspread beneath you;
Sing a hymn to the peak where Prometheus died
Still rising like a steeple through the air.
Know well that those who once fell
Like ashes on the earth, who long ago
Succumbed to the oppressors
Will rise again and soar, winged with hope,
Above the sacred mountain.
And as in bygone days
You glowed among the clouds,
Let your rays now play in splendour
Over the brilliant sky.
I shall tear like paper my silver blouse
And bare my breast to the moon
And with outstretched hands
Praise her who suckles the world with light.

for my mother, August 1895

(Freely adapted from Josef Stalin's second published poem, which appeared in the
liberal-progressive Georgian literary periodical Iveria, *October 1895.)*

2. ELEGY

Father, you will be for me always
The shadow of the onion spire chasing me home
Through dust at sundown up the Sobarnaya.
You will be for me always
The great drinker, great brawler whom men
Of our street defame since his departure
Without warning to a shallow grave. Father
You will be for me always
The cruel rhetorician, the bell-voiced preacher
Who made a plank table his pulpit, a fist his scripture,
A wife and child his battered congregation.
            You will be for me always
The onion spire that hung at your thighs
When you bathed, the virile aroma
Of your breath and body
Mortal as incense, foreign as the ikons
That made your room a forbidden chamber
Steeped in mysterious powers. Father
You will be for me always
Those black brows like a hawk's wings arching
Avid of prey, you will be for me beatings
We must have deserved
Though you would not give us a reason, Father,
You will be these things though you have left, you will stay
My teacher, my shadow, you
Drunk as a cobbler, boot-nails and brandy,
Hammer at the throat, you deity, Father,
I am nailed to the future
You will be for me always.

1896, for Vissarion (? – 1890)

3. ON READING DARWIN

From the shore I watched a cargo of chickens
Spill from a barge into the river.
Trapped in their wooden cages they floated
Momentarily in the freezing currents, then mutant
With fear, attacked one another, turned
Into fighting cocks, quarrelling,
Screeching, bleeding as their barred
Coffins filled with water.

From the riverbank I saw the bargemen
Forfeiting profit for a moment's diversion
And laughing at the disappearing birds
I thought of hungry schools
Of fish scuttling through the bars
Like the scoured ribs of drowned sailors
And white wings beating an idle descent
Through an evolving darkness.
From the riverbank I saw their feathers
Form alien words on the face of the waters;
At first I could not read them and I was afraid.

The seminary, 1896

4. EKATERINA

With her death the last shards of compassion in me
Are crushed. For too long I have squinted at the world
Through sheets of stained glass: the deep
Scarlet of sacrificial wounds, Christ's passion, the crimson
Fingers of a tyrant father. I walk from the churchyard
For the last time. Will you walk with me? I promise
We will not look back. No moving shade
Of pane could temper death's spectrum, or alter
The cast of my recollections. All dead. I regret everything
But the future. Walk beside me for your own good.
I shall drive histories before me like a flock of lambs.

1905

6. PHOTOGRAPH OF A GUTTED VILLAGE, GEORGIA

Should I be moved by this

Should I howl repentance and write poems
For the murdered comrade
And his wife, for the crippled child they would have beaten senseless
As soon as it could stumble

Should I dedicate psalms to the village mayor
Who slumped in the tavern every weeknight
Drunk, lecturing his witless electors,
Then tottering home to threaten his wife

Should I take up a collection
For the beggars who burned to death in the loft
Whose lives were a festering and a famishing
Who bred with the blind lust of dogs a line of stillborn sons

My comrade and his wife, the mayor, the village beggars,
Gone. This much, at least, I have corrected. You must understand
There are times these cratered vistas
Hold no nostalgia for me.
"Adorable Georgia"

Why should I be moved

Or weep and gather into my arms
The child squatting at the frame of the photograph, crooked
From beatings it took while still in the womb —

Perhaps it was the drunken mayor or his colleagues
Perhaps it was my murdered comrade
Whose brain at death hobbled back
Over its most brutal accomplishments, dreaming
Of blood as his eyes filled with it
Perhaps it was you my father, my father,
Why have you tormented me,
Twenty million times I have remembered

1922 (1949)

7. ELEGY IN EARLY WINTER

Nadezhda, it is snow they are calling for
from the Caspian Sea to Archangel.
And you are not here to see it.
With the rest of them you have disappeared
like the breath of old women at the doors
of cathedrals on Martyrs' Day, like a widow's prayers
in winter, hoof prints on the tundra,
whatever will not be sustained through time
or language. Your flesh
has proven snow, and like the rest of them
you melt: white cells and singular crystals
trampled, muddied by the stiff boots
of soldiers in Red Square. The Army, the Kremlin,
exiles and internees, all insubstantial
as myrrh from a censer, yellowing leaves
in the annals of the dead. My own being
is all I can credit. I am real. I do not melt.
And these others — tonight, these cumulous others —
the wireless crying out for snow
from the Black Sea to Archangel.

1932

9. TWO ELEGIES: A SON AND A COLLEAGUE

It will be said that now truly I have no people
because in Hitler I had found a kind of brother.
We held the same view of the dwarfs and freaks
who populate our earth with their squabbling litters,
for they are without ambition and therefore soulless.
    We have played for loftier stakes
and he has lost, though in his turn he made moves
that alarmed me, challenged me, made me stronger,
and took a son, my last true flesh, forever hostage.

from a letter, May 1945

11. "O POET, THE GEORGIANS HAVE PREPARED FOR YOU
A MONUMENT IN HEAVEN"

At six I could swim in the River Kura. My friends shouted
encouragement from the banks, though I knew they envied
my strength and courage. The Kura's cold, glinting current attracted
them but they were terrified of its darkness and depth. I was attracted
but not afraid. I was at home in the current, glad for the impassable
distance a few strokes could open between me and them. "Come
back, Soso," they would begin to shout. "Come back to shore."
And I would. On the banks we would wrestle until I threw
them, one after another, into the mild shallows, where they
thrashed and sputtered like apoplectics. Often I had to help
them out.

Though I was the smallest of our group I was admired and
feared and obeyed. Even then I sensed all around me an
impotence, a cosmic docility that deferred to the rich, the
strong, the determined. My family did not have money but I
was strong for my age and determined.

At seven I caught smallpox. My face after the affliction was
pocked and cratered as a battlefield, yet I found the disfigurement
strangely appealing. As if I had been wounded gravely in
some decisive conflict and was imperfectly healed; as if someone
had pressed from my skin small tokens of an invaluable metal.

The poems came much later, though I was still a boy when
I wrote them. They are perhaps a bit florid; I was filled at the
time with a sentimental affection for Georgia and her past. I
cherished the smells of the streets — from goat manure to
shashlik and rosewater sweets — and the way Gori looked
from the mountain under moonlight. I wanted to rip open my
shirt and bare my breast to the moon. I wanted to stretch out

my arms and worship the moon that showered the sleeping
earth with light. *Know well*, I sang, *that those*

Who long ago succumbed to the oppressors
Will rise again and soar, winged with hope,
Above the sacred mountain . . .

At seventy it occurs to me (in facetious moments) that I
have filled the sky thousands deep with soaring forms, there is
hardly room for them to manoeuvre, they collide and plummet
like massed cherubim in a religious tapestry. Though you
would not want to call them oppressed; they were and are as
vicious and debauched as the artists who prefigured them. I
crushed them to the last man.

And don't bother pointing self-righteously at certain lines
in my poetry; every author becomes a hypocrite with time. My
actions have annulled all juvenile hypocrisy by overwhelming it
with tides of actual blood. Ink is thin by contrast, the page pale.

A dictator is a poet of supreme accomplishments: his
words are always heard and he can make them mean whatever
he desires. He carves from the body of the world an order
hewn in his own image. A god does no more.

1949

12. DEATHBED DREAM

but gori from the mountainhead was lovely in sunlight
an old man with a black walking stick
let me taste his tobacco he had fought at sebastopol
against the english and french the wars he sang me
were full of flags in blue wind and polished brass and white
horses how the river kura shimmered at noon I would swim there
and people on the banks were clapping
to see a child in the water they had meat and bread in woven hampers
winebottles glittered like ice and the hot sun
lit up a face among many it was nadezhda
years before I met her watching from the banks as I reached out
I think she saw and toppled towards me into the river
disappearing quickly without a sign

FOREIGN GHOSTS (1990)

DEPARTURES

Like Bashō, I could set my mind to nothing.
I dreamed each night of islands, and the new moon
rising over Matsushima.
                              Days that summer
dump trucks lumbering past the fields
where I dug foundations for my father's house
churned dust from the sideroad, so that seams
of travelling particles darkened my skin. My lips,
rimed with the road-salt of layered winters,
tasted of a distant ocean.
I set down my spade.
                              This land,
my father told me once,
was buried under seas, these hills
a crowd of islands, terraced
over time with innumerable stories
I would never disinter, though I dug
through summer till I reached the bedrock,
filled a mandarin-crate with coins
and arrowheads, blank medallions, bottles
and pot-sherds — till I laid the foundations
of his house.
                              But like Bashō I was disturbed
from static labours by "spirits of the road," the foreign
ghosts spawning in salt dust
churned from turnpikes, and roused
by the prying shovel. That saw from childhood —
dig deep enough and you'll get to China.
I half-believed it possible
even after he'd explained to me,
No. A child kneeling in a sandbox

wilfully digging, unable to set his mind
to anything else.

A part of us
like a Japanese lantern drifts
on the surface of untold foreign lives;
these generations claiming hills of the world, a billionfold, your heart
in apparent exile. It means to find
the island it belongs to.

FOR PING HSIN, IN GOLMUD

Think of waking to cold
smells of clay walls, whatever's beyond them
must be waking to street scents, gutter
of flames from a brazier, clattering
cattle herded to slaughter sheds
outside further walls,
                              beyond this street
and the outskirts, horsemen
driving livestock outward,
behind them
                    stretch of plain to low hills,
beyond them
more hills and further hills and clay mountain
ranges beyond . . .

                    Think of elsewhere in clouds
and skies some time after, dry winds
at the slope of the world, squall
of stars, after words without
end, without meaning
beyond
            (rain in a desert where no one ——)
                                        these walls

SKY BURIAL

In Tibet the traditional form of funeral, "sky burial," involves hacking a corpse into pieces, which are left to the mountain birds. Soon only the bones remain; they are ground and mixed with the barley meal tsampa, *which was the person's staple in life and now constitutes a kind of soil to which the body is returned.*

Hide of stone slabs, slopes in mist
swooping down to temple yards
to a thousand small cairns like the graves of eagles;

by the mountain, birds soar in hungry loops,
mandalas in thin air, prayer kites
whirling before the plunge.

Each day somebody dies in Lhasa,
by dawn they are out to render him air,
give her to sky and birds that are the sky's hunger,

so as the thud of an axe tails off, and birds
coil downward in patient spools, you seem to see
a human form feathered on air — a figure

free at last to straddle updrafts off the mountain head,
slough hides of stone, grey slabs, slip free
of skin, as a monk at his dying might

hobble away from the monastery
that was never more than a phase and a preparation
into ascetic hills above the high plain,

above the cairns and scriptured cliffs,
to throw off like stained paper his maroon robes,
receive the wind.

FIRE BURIAL

The librarian monk is borne to his pyre
along the river, spring wind thrilling flames
as it cooled him in boyhood, fluttered pages

of his first reading. Consumed by those words
as now by fire, then wind sifting ash from shards
of spine (charred paper from its binding),

he expected and desired this burning
conclusion, believed he was a coffer
in each current of his thought, knew in the end

that a sacred book, like any scarred body,
Buddha of clay or the monastery itself,
was a medium only: beauty

honoured him with use, and flowing through him
like wind in a brief passage, murmuring,
referred him to the fire.

THE BRAIDING

Pokhara

When she braids her hair above me, three strands
twined into one, it hurts slightly
as if she held veins or open nerves, as if
my whole body were one strand, clenched
between her fingers.

She must be another strand,
I guess, as sometimes when she pulls
she winces, her startled exhalation
a warm gust across my chest.

And as the braid comes to be
between her fingers, and the difficult
knot is tied, I wonder
about the last strand,
the biggest, woven between us
like the fact of a former lover — or

no, I'd say now, more like
the new being two bodies
form in their joining —
which is a way of seeing love,
the newborn ghost
that lives inside this trinity.

UNFINISHED BUDDHA, SAMED ISLAND

Eyes at the level of palm-fronds
above the clearing, half-closed, gaze
from a jail of rotten scaffolding. Here jungle
completes a job, closes like a membrane
over the sand's blank stare; at ankles
scrub lashes, drags like an undertow.

The figure is only half-complete —
facial features coarse and hard
as if not yet enlightened, no
fingers carved free of the concrete
stubs of hands, the folds of the sarong
undelved and the skin, rough
as stucco, blemished with birth-
marks of accidental paint.

No monks, you can see, have worked here
for some time. The priory has aged in a quiet
trance of decline, most of the inmates long since
dead or returned to the city.
                          But the Buddha remains,
marooned like those busts on Easter Island
and likewise caught in a timeless half-
blink, as if stunned to find himself stranded
by his sculptors, his parish, his own priests.
And his fixed, androgynous half-smile
has less to do with peace, or perfect stillness,
than with the bafflement you might perceive
some day at a mirror, your own scaffolding
of belief stripped away, you left on the shrinking
islet of a clearing, unfinished, unfreed,
while all your rituals return to sand.

CEREMONY FOR ANCESTORS, KŌYA SAN

They said *Burn with an inside flame*
like Japanese lanterns
we would see each other clearly

Burn away the fingered ribs containing
a flammable heart, burn away
the wrinkled tissue, we would see this much, at least,
of our flesh and family —

                    "I recognize you,"
a stranger said. "I think I do. Your father's
living image. I suppose
he must be here
tonight?"
            I told him no.
                    Tonight
candelabra of children amble
among stars, follow the trails of flame
calling parents
and calling them, calling them
to suppers by the tomb, by candle, they said
Burn
Burn away
that part of us our children, even,
could not have seen
                    Burn what they might discover
                    Burn what they might infer: flames' real tints,
the urn in ribs that lived
that death we held inside us —

                    They told me, "Look

with the eye's wick ignited
into forest behind the tombs
up the bird-encircled mountain
Look
your mother is that gravid darkness
urging you to burn"

       I didn't answer —
we are the living, we must suffer
the obscure vigils of the dead —

and eyes pressing from the forest,
voices at the river's source catch flame
in the world's cold furnace

         Burn

Mother, father, you cindering
fuse of my flesh and hours, you too are foreign
ghosts, and I am
haunted by your absence.

        Japanese lanterns along a bridge
cast in the water reflections
like the moon, repeated, years in a mirror
a face you do not know.

NAKUNARU

In the Japanese language *to die*
is to become invisible, to be lost,
to go missing
             so when Hideyuki Murata disappeared
in the August blast, scoured
from a street in the core of Nagasaki
             haunting the upper air as atoms of heat
or energy mingled with cinders
             of his wife and children, winnowing
down into fields along the coast

             so when he disappeared, it seemed
his language had already prepared
a vocabulary to deal with his loss

             And when Hideyuki went
with his 75 years, he took
these things with him:
             the singular bluegreen
his eyes made of bays east of Shimabara
when he first fished there with his uncle
             the way the paddy field by his house
had smelled in the summer heat, like rice
steaming, nearly cooked,
his mother's voice calling him to supper
             a freak snow one April, melted down
by noon, the tart
stab of a crabapple
biting into his tongue, a best friend shot beside him
at Mukden, 1905

his first monsoon his father dead
and a woman kissed him —

        and old eyes noting in wind
over the harbour, a single
silver gleam — a seagull maybe
flying inland, catching the early light

and disappearing
with a toll of thunder
into remarkable cloud

NATIONAL MUSEUM, KYŌTO

1

HAKEGAWA, Kiyoshi (1926–)

Oiseau sur un livre (nature morte) and

pencil on canvas, it appears
the young woman stopped before it is lost
in meditation, does the flatness and

nightmare detachment of shapes
disturb her, draw her
in, or

is she (shifting now, hand
flitting at hair)
              adjusting her
self, criticizing

the makeup that ran, in the ideally black
background she sees her own shadow
enter the frame

2

Nine months here and only this
museum view
of moon through a spider's web

THE ECSTASY OF SKEPTICS (1994)

PROLOGUE

Divorce was a hooded, shadowy caller
armed with a briefcase instead of a scythe.
Back then he paid house calls to so many
families in our neighbourhood
so come nightfall, bedtime, the brittle, bare
staircase by my room would screech and
jitter and rumble with my fear he would come,
had come, to see us.

        He never called.

              Yet the stairs
kept creaking, twelve teeth of a saw, jig-
sawing the soft place where I dreamed
into a labyrinth of forks and junctures, seeing my father
was English, my mother Greek
and so different,

        and though they gave no sign
they would ever ask him in, I was afraid
that one night gliding past us on his rounds
he would sniff out the hybrid, oddball
energies of our house
and with empty X-ray sockets, home in
on dotted lines of tension in the walls
and with bony finger pick the locks,
and my parents, loud in argument or love,
wouldn't hear a thing
till he'd swept up behind and his briefcase
had sprung open like a cobra's jaws
and our lives were vacuumed in.

            Home
for us was no womb but a crucible, a carnival

51

of masks, mouths carved in every mood,
a melting pot full of hail and grapeleaves
that would never boil down to one — to nothing —
or feed the hooded guy.
                    Home —
where any table and page is, and I pen them
together in a room again: close the paper
door of the notebook and leave them
face to face,
                    still talking —

BIRTHDAY

Mornings, the sunbeams' flowing escalator drew up
at your mother's door, drew up
your eyes and weaned them from the damp
verandah while, nine months new, you crawled
under the window where your mother baked. Called

and called to at ten months, you pressed on, turtled
down steps to the garden — bold turtle
without a shell, back damp
with dew from drooping poppies, as if wet
from the egg, and your mother must have felt

a tugging, a pang at the navel
as if the scalpel never sheared your navel,
as you pulled away from her into the damp
and drying world, a third eye in the belly you both
once saw from — when? — welling damp with

sweat, fear's scalpel at the heart
sawing, stabbing . . . A month older and her heart
could hardly stand the laughter as you in your damp
bulging trousers tried to stand
until, for a moment, you *stood*, and never mind

that two steps later you tumbled in the sun
or that a month later in the autumn sun
you'd still be falling — to her, at the door, hands damp
with frosting, you'd roamed beyond all reeling back,
though even now she recalls you for the cake

she holds in the doorway, calling!
  calling! while years away in the roses you break
      and bury her heart in the garden,
          to grow.

PORTRAIT OF A FATHER

I dreamed his head was floating on the sea
and said these words   *Leave the forest*
for the sun's shore, for Apollo   the body
is a hallowed cannibal: noon is best,

quit the cult of the pulse and the wine-beams
bleeding like war from the moon's barrel. (The rest
was swallowed with a roar, as the sea
opened, whale-wide.
                              I woke up.)
                                        In other dreams
he's carried out past saving on his own brain-waves,
body blue as an embryo, a glacier, in a blank sea
never free of signs: the passing sails

hold sonnets, the horizon, electric with heart-waves,
hums, and the eye is a diving bell plunged through the sea
to where the sun's silver machinery fails.

ELEGY AS A MESSAGE LEFT ON AN ANSWERING MACHINE

Hello, you've reached 542-0306. I'm unable to answer the phone just now, but just leave a message after the beep and I'll be sure to return your call.

Goodbye for now

***

Won't bother waiting up for you
to get back to me on this one. Waste of time.
My dime
in a bar by the water, your factory-new

answering machine is — like anything bereaved — still
full of your words, the waves
of your voice, the nervous laugh that gave us,
sometimes, "cause" to laugh. And which we now miss. Well,

human nature. I say Fuck my own. I own
up: this stinks. Too late
to erase all the crap, a Watergate
of gossip, off-hand words, no time to phone-

in those last-minute changes, additions, to say
what we find so impossible to say —
I find. So cut all this *can't*
come to the phone right now cant, I don't

buy it, I figure you're in there somewhere, still
screening your calls, you
secretive bastard, pick up the phone now if you
would hear a friend. Don't stall,

don't, like me. Thinking
there's time, still time enough, or rather
not thinking enough. Now look, I'm not sure whether
the executors will be disconnecting

you — your line — tomorrow (nurses, almost, pulling closed
the green curtain and tearing
out of your torso the drips and plugs and electrodes
to leave you drifting

with that astronaut in the film
who squirms awhile, signals some last, frantic word
then spins away into the void) —
that's why I'm here. Sky's clear tonight, by the way, calm

the wind, the water. Not sure really
why I called —
gesture of a drunk old
friend and ally.

Anyway it was pretty good
for a second or two, to
get through,
Tom,

goodbye.

LONG DISTANCE EVERY SIGN

Long distance every sign —
another poem the road gave you.
Another song the aerial
sucked out of sound waves into the car
far gone
on the freeway filed to sand behind your tires
or the forest trail growing in behind you
or the paddles' footprints, fading
in a bay at dawn, as ice knits closed after your stern
and keeps pace

At the wheel could you feel above you
the sun's wheel turn
and shuttle you into darkfall, home, and see
the dashboard's green galaxies at dusk
evolving, burning, and by dawn
burnt down

I want to wake at the wheel still driving
somehow changed, want you there beside me
as the road hairpins like a heartline, climbing
and we near another elsewhere
want you there at the wheel, at the wheel
I still believe
for as long as it turns
I can clutch the sun I can steer and
brake time to a hold

These times I still believe in every poem the road gave me
though at daybreak they shrink away
like a distance every sign, and the road

that seemed by night a bare arm
unbroached by any watch, and reaching
clear into dawn, emerges

Mondayed —
bone-beige —
manacled with quartz —

                        a scar in the suburbs
of a clock-skulled place.

AN ELEGY, YEARS AFTER SARAH

So her ceiling a map of stars. First time we made love
late afternoon late winter, and after as she slept
how her room fogged up with dusk
and paper stars she'd stuck up there in childhood
came out in strange constellations
and I missed the earth
till her room was night her breath deepening the stars
cooling down: I said *come closer* and her eyes
— half-open, flashing back whatever light there was — went out.

CONVERSATION IN A GALLERY

The exhibition halls were deserted. Occasional guards
dozed awkwardly at their posts
like unfinished statuary. It seemed it hardly
mattered what I stole or took the trouble to deface.

In a viewing room I thought I'd almost
stumbled on another visitor: it was actually a life-
sized statue, set in place
before a wall of staring portraits. Art

paying attention to art. Life
imitates nothing without our eyes, and finally ghosts
all we do with a fine film of soil
or dust — and yet

as at a conference of adepts (art-
scholars, psychologists, or the collectors
of china or rare insects) there is this traffic
between dignified stone heads or heads in dry oil

in a dialect no one else knows, which is therefore
silent. Silent, as this gallery is now
with its long row of reluctant jurors
who are going to have to accept the coming verdict

and really you would like to know

how for so long these desiccated gazes drew you
into a fool's auction, and sold you
their hourglass shares of time-
past and time-future

in exchange for all your currency
          — in exchange for perfect rhymes and resonant conceits
that might survive the moment or the era
the inconvenience of, say, a lover or a child is
nothing, they whispered
          for what seemed a long time
I paid attention to their words
while the wordless trials of a lover turned the room
into a ghost-gallery of cases, closed,
and I paid and I paid and I paid.

SLOW LIGHTNING

a scholar as child

Four years brought a sunrise of memory
in a beam of light descending a stairwell
lined with ancestral faces. Now I see them, baffled
under glass, trapped behind iron
bars of sunlight from the forge
of a star much older, cooler than their own.
Their lips and hair, pale sepia skin
all like my father's, flickering
on the memory's screen, the blank back of the skull
where I still see the door
of his study swing ajar, his body
in the threshold a guardian, his teeth
grinning like a chain of keys.

And when I went in: dim shelves refuting the faint
light trailing me from the door, desk of rosewood,
broad-backed chair, so many books my head reeled
when I tried to count them. And trying to reckon
with the room's seductions I went in again
and again, a moth caught by the spidery light
of print on bindings, or pulled
by the vortex from a bonfire of volumes
burning in a city square.
                              When he caught me
he said nothing, led me out with soft, compositor's hands
more used to a book's brittle spine — and the door behind us
shut like a cover. So we stood outside
in the cold passage, hand-in-hand, and as I grew

to fill his absence he held me fast, those portraits
fading, my father gone, and still
on the carpeted stairway
the sunbeam
fell,
　　　slow lightning.

IN HERACLITUS'S CITY

Begin like sisters with fingers linked, the city
and the sea, quayed where the marble street would end
two thousand years back, and every year since then
for the length of a long bone the sea has been

crawling off and moss darkening the dead-end
cobbles with a caul of green, so now the jetty,
broken, reaches — seems to reach — out to a receding
far-off fingertip of the Aegean. These hours

that sand down faces, bury vows in desert graves and send
sisters to scattered time zones, bereave us
of our harbours; in the tumbled senate, wind

has the last civil word, while melodramatic above the ruins
the theatre spreads out its great robed arms
and after twenty centuries can say nothing.

REWRITING THE DEAD

What we glimpse of her now is less
than the frozen trickle of light from a star
extinct since the Pharaohs' age

yet flickering. Every hour the familiar eyes
get fainter, the form less clear; the living
come to revise her words, like cousins

contesting a will, and claiming
who she loved most, most favoured — who she
failed to praise — who she failed. The dead

are a newfound planet, drifting,
distant as Neptune's moons, but colonized
quickly, gridded with myth, their bones

embellished like the relics of saints —
each breath they're less themselves and more
like satellites in a galaxy, born

of need and speculation. Because we must
we rewrite the dead — bind them in silence and dust-
jackets of soil, of pine. Soon enough their souls

become too frail to slip
the gravity of defining words, and fail
to check our sloppy captions. So they don't point out

how we absolve them of their being
and replace them, soon, the way a stellar
hologram might be flashed on the sky

the moment the Pharaohs' star blinks out.

GLOSA

I wept when I remembered
How often you and I
Had tired the sun with talking
And sent it down the sky

— Kallimachus, fl. N. Africa c. 350 BCE

You were careful, at the first brush of the wing,
not to put anyone out. The pain and numbness
kicked in at dawn; you waited till 9:15 — not 9 —
to call your doctor. He told you
Heart attack. Get yourself down to Hotel Dieu, Emergency, fast. Tom,
you walked. You walked the mile and a bit — you lumbered,
really, side to side, because, you said, your legs
felt leaden, your head light, your heart tightening like a drawstring sack.
Who held the strings? For three days none of us heard.
I wept when I remembered

how you'd tried not to put us out, how we only
found you by chance, then abashed you with visits, vases
filled with the clover and scilla flourishing then
in your own, overgrown yard. Mild, you said —
you said the experts pronounced it mild, and you fine.
You looked fine. Just cut the booze, you said, the bacon and eggs. Try
to remember your pills, all seventeen of them,
though you only mentioned a couple, and we only
found the others later. Now, looking back, I'm surprised by
how often you and I

did get together, despite everything, the busyness, the dead-
lines down every hall, lasers in a rigged house; how a single man
comes to cave in on himself, like a house untended, his ego

an armchair in the wreckage, the staved-in windows
jagged, so the hand tendered in or out
never quite arrives. Yet we did get together and I managed, walking
beside you through a city of fractures (prison and prepschool,
earth/river/lake), to see the patient friend in you break
surface in your eyes, though it seemed you weren't listening,
had tired the sun with talking,

were ready to retire to that armchair, where no babbling
novice irked you with his table talk. Well, sure.
I know the feeling. How you didn't — didn't seem to —
listen. Tom,
          listen now: last night I dreamed a tree was growing
out of your house, branching through each window and door, scraping
clear of the skylight, as scilla might blaze up through an eyesocket
in the earth. There were leaves, and the delicate skeletons
of small birds hung in wind-chimes off the boughs. Their marrow
was music, like yours now — song. Off the cliff of my tongue I made the
      music fly
and sent it down the sky.

THE BED *(a letter)*

A week before boarding ferries
for separate ports, we found a bed
in the orchard above the inn,
abandoned. How many falls?
Dead leaves curled together
by the headboard, wind
snoring in the olive trees.
That mattress, gutted, where mice
had hollowed out their feather rooms —
their catacombs.
                  Beneath the road
the gorge was filled with the greening
relics of buses, cars; dark shrines
roosted above us like ravens
in the hillside.

And the rain. Did I forget
to mention it? Well,
we've had some more.

Just yesterday I saw it fall
through a bone-dry morning
onto islands off the coast.

EPITAPH, UNFINISHED

From a two-line fragment, dyslexically scrawled in the notebook of a
crewman from the disastrous Franklin Expedition of 1845–48[?]. The
notebook was found by a search party, in 1854, beside the remains of an
unidentified sailor who had been involved in the crew's doomed march
south towards the mainland.

Oh Death whare is thy sting, the grave
At Comfort Cove for who has any doubt now . . . the dyer
Said . . . Whare is thy victory

In cairns by a seacoast none sails, whare the point
In nought returning now the year's Spring
When Kings go forth, our ship a Jonah in the white jaws of

What Season this? What Easter
& the ship unmanned behind by God I
saw some slip bone-anchor through a wheezing

porthole of the sea; saw souls so trudged by the cross of labour
Rope-burn Wind-burn Eyes blind at barely Noon
each body, — lean — a sundial aimed at
     aimed at

         How sting of gravel horned us, boots
stuffed for the storm with pages, teared
from prayer-books *I shall not want*
    Here in a horde of poor devils in the wilderness, whare Christ
tempts &

           taunts us

                              Ah
              one sprig of larksong & gladly I
          should slow as my ink & wander a
                              way from the dying lines:

alone.   to the parched hymn of
                         Is it grey,   gunbarrel
                    breakers beating Judgement?

                                        See

see how they Fall   each frothing crest by

                    Christ a palm   a Finger

                                   pointing into,

HIKERS

It's always best to walk behind
other hikers on the trail, or follow
tracks into thick forest, where narrow
crooks and blinds distract the eye

so the moment's stride is all you know
and the woods conceal the coming rise —
that sheer grade, like a sleepless night,
always close to ending. But what if it showed —

if we could picture the paths of our life
scrambling over scree, up the treeless meadows
and the balding ridge, until the body is slowed
by thin air and age, and draws near the divide?

Much better for some to come behind
through the blind, dense forest, with heads bowed.

PSALM: FOR THE WIND & THE SHIELD COUNTRY

The wind is my shepherd, and I must walk
Where it drives me until day's end.
It guides me into barren hills
More beautiful than gardens, at dark
It leads me to lie
Under sheets of rain, it feeds me
The warm wafer of the sun
Steaming from dawn's embers. I am drawn down
By the wind's fingers to waters
That are never still, my staff
And compass are the living boughs, the leaves
My roof, my shifting floor,
                                        and I must live
Like the mountain, briefly
And always, in wide
Mansions of the wind.

A PSALM, ON SECOND THOUGHT

      I'm not afraid of taking this harp
down from the willow
to sing — though no one
trusts song much any more, or the singer —
      and sometimes this harp is a hacksaw, my fibres
pulsating to notes
a living ash might make when carved
my words are warrants
my metre martial
my pacifist slogan a summons to war
      I've confused, at times, orders
for order, I've psalmed orchards
loaded with lush plump fruit and not
the prison walls behind, chanted
Carmanesque Shield Country isles while acid
suds censored the lee shore, said *barren*
hills more beautiful than gardens — ignoring
the tools or tailings that
made them so.
            I'm not afraid of easing this harp
out of the limbs of the dying
willow to sing, but who can sing, and not become
the laureate of a state
of legislated greed?
               And if my tongue forget?

                    I'm afraid

at times,
      of taking this harp
down from the dead
willow to sing

in a valley of tailings

the wind

was my ward, orphaned, my failing

garden of air, &

goodness &

mercy

will surely

all the days of my

TAKAYAMA *(a dream in Japanese)*

You feel, so far inland,
    in a seabird's midnight cry
        the loss of a baby daughter.

*

By the river, where paper houses
perch on stilts like herons
in a rising tide, I sit
and dangle feet in currents
white as milk with melted snow, and wait
till the river rises through my emptiness, fills
my belly my heart my breasts, and breaks
in ocean brine from my eyes.

*

Why did you leave me
for the open sky?
Clouds rise too
but in a fall of snow
return to the earth.

STONE MOUNTAIN ELEGY

for Chris Wiseman

In April, winds off the glacier
blow between stones of a graveyard
in the mountains. Here your mother is
buried, and you've asked us to come,
leave flowers, clean the site, bring

news that all is . . . what? Peaceful, I suppose.
In its place, not vandalized, not quite
vanished. And everything is all right —
everything is fine. We leave a vase,
clean the plot, bow faces, pace

among stones, but as the others head
for the fence it strikes me I'm afraid
to let you know what a small thing
a stone is in the mountains. No
matter how tall, how elaborate,

it's always shadowed by the great
shrugged shoulder of the range — I guess
when you were here you must have seen?
I could tell you, too, how faults
in the mountain spell out names in snow

(names no one can ever read, or say)
but you must know that too. When
was the last time you travelled west?
Ten years? Twenty? How they pass . . .

And the small stones seem to whisper now
what was it kept you away?

WERE YOU TO DIE

Were you to die I'd be free to go off
and see the world, and sleep in every elsewhere
I might never arrive
— yet I might choose to travel alone
from window to window looking out
on the streets of your city,
where your friends still expect to see you sometimes
or mistake you for someone, out of custom, love.

Without your thrashing, manic dreams, my body
would sleep better
but wake more tired, I'd let the garden go to seed
the way I always meant to
and when I looked out the window into the yard
I'd never miss the snowpeas, beets and roses
but your sunhat I might miss — you hunkered down
in a summer dress, your fingers
grouped like roots in the raised beds,
your stooped, stubborn nape, your cinnamon-
freckled shoulders.

Were you to die, my heart
would be free to pack a bag
and book passage for the riot of islands
I might have been, and shared
with the one and numberless "beloved" we fumble
our whole lives glimpsing
a moment too late,
when Eden was always the one who stayed
rooted in her changes, and gave you
the island in her arms, and when you slept

somehow she travelled, and when you woke
she was changed.

Were you to die, my mind
would be free to twist inward
the way fingers fist, and fasten pat
on its own taut notions, theorems, palm shut fast
to the snow that pooled there and seemed to flow through
when the skin still flowered in fullest winter
and I loved you, and thoughts, like books,
were doors that opened outward,
not coffins, closed,
not cells.

Were you to die and free me
my body would follow you down into the cold
prison of your passing, to warm you
when all the others had turned away, and try
bribing the keeper with a poem, or fool him
with keychains of chiming words — an elegy
so pure he'd be pressed to cry, eyes
thawing and the earth warmed, April
when rain falls like a ransom, through opened arms
that bore the sun down with you, warm.

THE ECSTASY OF SKEPTICS

EXIT signs in the scholars' hallway
Lead through polished sheets of plate glass
Into air into thin air —

                    outborne
From an ivory silence
Where the world was to be rephrased,
Where the skeleton key of learned
Rigour cracks
Feckless in the lock, where screens
Glow green as chlorophyll (or
Landfill, breeding — a Babel
Of cavilled, rootless words that mean,
In the heart's hearing, what?)

                    This tongue
is a moment of moistened dust, it must learn
to turn the grit of old books
into hydrogen, and burn
The dust of the muscles must burn
down the blood-fuse of the sinews, the tendons'
taut wick, these bones like tinder giving light
to read by, and heat, the winter light is already
lagging, we'll soon be less than cinders, adrift
in an aftermath of space . . .

Voices in the scholars' hallway
lead through fastened doors
into catacombs of jargon, parchment hives.

Now, love. This way. With the lights on. Blazing.

THE ADDRESS BOOK (2004)

For everyone
The swimmer's moment at the whirlpool comes

— Margaret Avison

I loved so many people everywhere I went —
Some too much, and others not enough.

— Woody Guthrie

ADDRESS BOOK

Bad luck, it's said, to enter your own name
and numbers in the new address book.
All the same, as you slowly comb
through the old one for things to pick

out and transfer, you are tempted to coin
yourself a sparkling new address,
new name, befitting the freshness of this clean-
slating, this brisk kiss

so long to the heart-renders — every friend
you buried or let drift, those Home for the Aged
maiden relations, who never raged
against the dying of anything, and in the end

just died. An end to the casualties pressed
randomly between pages — smudged, scribbled chits
with lost names, business cards with their faded
bold fronts of confidence, solvency. The palimpsest

time made of each page; the hypocrite it made
of you. Annie, whom you tried two years to love
because she was straight-hearted, lively, and in love
with you (but no strong-arming your cells and blood);

Mad Carl, who typed poet-to-poet squibs in the pseudo-
hickish, hectoring style of Pound, all sermonfire
and block caps, as AINT FIBRE ENOUGH HERE, BOYO,
BACK TO THE OLE FLAX FIELD . . . this *re* a score

of your nature poems. When he finally vanished
into the far east, you didn't mind the silence.
Still, this guilt, as if it weighs in the balance,
every choice—as if each time your pen banished

a name it must be sensed somewhere, a ballpoint stab, hex-
needle to the heart, the treacherous
innocent *no* of Peter, every X
on the page a turncoat kiss . . .

Bad luck, it's said, to enter your own name in the new
book — as if, years on, in the next culling,
an executor will be leafing through and calling
or sending word to every name but you.

THE AMERICAN NIGHT LISTENS

His longing, strung on the American night, knew its own slavage.
Debt-peon to such lean solitudes. *Drink with me, please.*
Precious friend, you cannibal of elders, your maimed
shoes, lager-lame step, made a hundred-storied ledge
of any sidewalk: hesitation-cut cracks. Forgive me this
going. I always miss you. You thought your uncombed
thoughts and spoke them, penned dense letters so
manically amped and you still must, I guess,
for others somewhere. We two in the post-party
dark as MacGowran does *Malone Dies*, and the lines
of stereo lights are a landing field below, blinking red
in fog. How your mind then seemed a soaring lamp.
Tell me something important, you said (drunk, dead
drunk again), and I was stumped. Friend, I still am.

THE WOOD OF HALFWAY THROUGH

A daughter

Any forest craves torrents
of breeze in noon's steeper blaze: as a glider
seeks thermals coiled into high currents,
each aerial a ladder

into middle air. Appearance
never speaks for marrow. I think I was sadder
before you than friends saw. Now all my *aren'ts*
and *shouldn'ts* recede, I'm the reader

of a tongue lacking the negative mood,
the conditional, and other places to hide.
Who is it loves you, his heart now a lantern

in the dark wood of halfway through? The one
you made solid when he felt himself shade,
who made his way back from the border, made good.

CONSTELLATIONS

After bedtime the child climbed on her dresser
and peeled phosphorescent stars off the sloped
gable-wall, dimming the night vault of her ceiling
like a haze or the interfering glow
of a great city, small hands anticipating
eons as they raided the playful patterns
her father had mapped for her — black holes now
where the raised thumb-stubs and ears of the Bat
had been, the feet of the Turtle, wakeful
eyes of the Mourning Dove. She stuck those paper
stars on herself. One on each foot, the backs
of her hands, navel, shoulders, tip of nose,
then turned on the lamp by her bed and stood close
like a child chilled after a winter bath
pressed up to an air duct or a radiator
until those paper stars absorbed more light
than they could hold. Then turned off the lamp,
walked out into the dark hallway and called.

Her father came up. He heard her breathing
as he clomped upstairs preoccupied, wrenched
out of a rented film just now taking grip
on him and the child's mother, his day-end
bottle of beer set carefully on the stairs,
marking the trail back down into that evening
adult world — he could hear her breathing (or
really, more an anxious, breathy giggle) but
couldn't see her, then in the hallway stopped,
mind spinning to sort the apparition
of fireflies hovering ahead, till he sensed
his daughter and heard in her breathing

the pent, grave concentration of her pose,
mapped onto the star-chart of the darkness,
arms stretched high, head back, one foot slightly raised —
the Dancer, he supposed, and all his love
spun to centre with crushing force, to find her
momentarily fixed, as unchanging
as he and her mother must seem to her
and the way the stars are; as if the stars are.

2001, AN ELEGY

First scene:
   I was the child
plucked from Miss Porch's kiln of a second grade
classroom, Indian summer 1968, the getaway Datsun
panting at the curb, Dad at the wheel — and you, like Jackie O,
with gangland shades and auburn bouffant, gold
drachma profile, making me your merry truant,
secret suitor. And for a matinee. (Miss Porch,
I think, subsequently disapproved.)
Decades later you would recall nothing of this,
and then, at the closing, nothing at all.
But the film lingers. How HAL's robotic voice
resembled Vice-Principal Hoop's ominous monotone,
Just what do you think you're doing . . . Dave . . .
and the spacemen in their plastic hibernacula
as futuristic pharaohs, LIFE FUNCTIONS
TERMINATED . . . and how, for thirty-three years,
that science-fiction date "2001" reared, monolithic
though distant as Jupiter, black parsec-stone or
postmodern tower, where I'd make it
to forty years, my parents
a Paleolithic sixty-five.

Later scene:
   The deep space of Mount Pleasant
Theatre smudged with sweet, unfamiliar fumes
(unlike the Pall Malls you're smoking) and I press close,
peer up as Kubrick's chromatic vortices make violent
kaleidoscopes of your cat-eye lenses, the capsule
like a pill plummets through psychedelic voids, and

you and Dad (I think now) wonder if maybe
Fantasia would have been better . . . Now see the hero,
retired, sexless, mummified in his final bed —
hard to conceive, from inside the living
frame of family, such mythic age
and solitude. There are losses beyond losing.
The one closing I never foresaw:
that 2001 would be your year to leave, and me
in the "dark wood" of halfway through, commuting
fear to fear, until I reach your cribside (yes,
just that) and recite — since hearing's always last
to lapse — your favourite Hopkins — *I desired to go*
where springs not fail, where flies no . . .

Cotside. Coffinside. *Wait for me wait for me*
wait for me the widower said —

Closing scene:
                    Bed in a white room
where I sit by your side for a last *again*, read you more,
No sharp and sided hail, and a few lilies blow.
From a lampless house in high-flung fallow
you've the metropolis for starfields, high-beams
of cars on concession roads cruising slow
and straight as satellites, space probes.
                                        In New Year's
smallest hours, you find a child deep inside
your hearing, murmuring, *Mama,*
listen. It's 2001.
We made it.

FROM A HIGHER WINDOW

There was no night in that night.
The moon soldiered through the smog.
The rails so near your bedside window
you both smelled the cigarettes of engineers
with diesel drafts, steel wheels stammering
the last, brakes-on stage to the port, shaking
the bedframe, swivelling ambulance strobes
across your ceiling.
                  He tells you that he used to love
being the one who loves less. Believe him,
leave on the lamp. Let tired trainmen wonder
why it burns so late, in a blue window, crepe
curtains alive there like a negligee drying
in the crude breath of engines arriving from the east.
(They haul sunrise behind them out of the Rockies,
a whole dry summer in their cars.)
Don't let him doze. Lie to him
that this, and he, are the only best, tonight
in your boxcar of a room, floating
high over the sleepers on their bed of stones,
where you both out-sing the trains.

LOST WATERFALLS

For the strangled impulse there is no redemption
                — Patrick Kavanagh

There was a waterfall, mapped in the founding
survey, two hundred years ago and lost,
eroded—something—so no later crew,
miner, or bushwalker has seen a thing.
                                 The river
it should have ruptured is still there, unspooling
where it ought to, out of the Burnt Hills down through timber
east of the Perth Road, chattering with chipped
fossils, flint-shards sparked by eels, then pooling
in a colonnade of cedars where the lost
falls should be exploding, still.

Went looking for you, what I thought was you.
A skirling of wind in the skymost branches
and peering round me for the radiant detonation,
vapours pulsing up from the sinkpool, I seem
to see the chalk-white shock of it — a cliffslide
through the cedars' warped, ashen balusters —
almost feeling the mist of this vision
condensed to a strange dew's
trickle down my face.

Wind dwindles then, dies, and that ghost-foam
flickers, the cataract-roar ebbs to the dodder
of a stone-bald, greying, oblivious river,
and I go.

Where have you got to? Gone to. Two hundred years,
the path healed over, the cedars deadfallen
or deeper in the sky, the mapmakers
deeper in the ground.
                    There is a waterfall, they lied,
afraid that love dries to a dotted line
on the map, that the river in time
slips underground, and   *This to prove*
we were loved. This whim
against what drifts to dark.

We know, of course, it will not be found.

DRUNK JUDGEMENT

A night address

The world is wasted on you. Show us one time
beyond childhood (or the bottle) you spent your *whole*
self — no blood-bank back-up, some future aim
to fuel — or let yourself look foolish, freestyle
on barstool, backstreet, dancefloor, without a dim
image of your hamming hobbling you the while.
Voyeur to your couplings, you never did come
with them, did you, even when you did? You said Hell
is details, when Hell was the cave, the concave-
mirrored skull you dwelt inside, your left hand
polishing while the right shook to clinch a deal —
Provide, provide! Sure, in the end, like any soul
you were endless *and yets* — brave, deft with phrases, kind —
three cheers for you. Too closed to want what others love
you vetoed life —
     were there other worlds to crave?

MAPS OF THE TOP OF THE WORLD

New moon — a starveling
  curled on blue earth and quickly
    swallowed by snowdrift clouds —

Late in *The Lure of the Labrador Wild*
the solemn falling of snow in the firwood, the
famine-wood, and before long sly, soft winds
till drifts oversift the tomb of the tent
like an A-frame in a snowbelt storm

— and inside that canvas husk
a smaller husk now exempt from struggle, the ardent
anomalies of consciousness, animal heat
and shunted blood. Sink now sleep a fugue
of crackling maps, wistful misnamings echoing
in talus-grey defiles —
                    Providence Point
                    Cape Homer
                    Homeward Cove —
                              of firepits

once more warmly
antlered with flame.

              The explorer's dream
is just the yearning of doomed
molecules for eternity, ancient urge
to impregnate barrens with menhirs,
cairns and runes, with
ruins,

and you there likewise,

                    Purdy,

in your oxygen tent,

               mind off elsewhere

                           stumbling in a blizzard

of drugs —

        you too came this far,
imprinted the ice shelves and foolscap floes
of how many blank sheets
and pharmacy notebooks,

                    wanted to "do the country"
so you kept afoot, always moving
against the stasis to come, always
talking back at the silence to come

                        and at that final forecloser,
repossessor, who serves the body
such intimate writs, gives pressing notice
that each breath is borrowed, the warmed and
wobbling space you occupy
is leased —

And maybe all this movement and exploration is really
in hopes of finding — founding — some new "Vinland
the Good"
             somewhere out beyond
all vital eviction, where poets, friends,
like dogged squatters in life's rickety A-frame
vie and recite over homebrew, wild grape wine,
with invincible livers on a pine-box patio
that never will sag further than this

— and the day holds, hovering at the late August hour
of light's most inebriate angle, on the relic
phonograph Paul Robeson revived to the lap
and backbeat of lake-waves, woodwind breezes
through the weeping willow's green marquee,
and the old rowboat is straked and caulked so that later
a few might row it across to the brook mouth
and alongside the pioneer graveyard, knowing
its bottomless appetite is finally sated
and the living forever barred . . .

He loved the poetry of place-names most
and set them down accordingly —

So sink now sleep a fugue
of crackling maps, wistful misnamings
signposted in permafrost

                        Ft Good Hope
                        Mt Somerset
                        Pt Victory

the pit of the belly
once again warmly
furnaced with flame

                   and "know where the words came from"

THE LAST LIVING SPEAKER OF THE ARONDHA TONGUE
CAUGHT ON VIDEO A FEW HOURS BEFORE HER DEATH

Her pauses lengthening, the abyss
between phrases like the faults between
a heart's ragged, forceless
beating on an

ECG. A fickle
flickery line that seems to chart
the country of her people —
its tablelands, tors, inert

streambeds and saltwaste
cratered round. Except that the bone-
sown soil was never the ghost-
green of this electric line,

its vital tines now fainter, fewer.
Is she revisiting that flower
said to blossom a single night
per century? They knew where to wait

and why. Mind-mapped each chant-line,
glyph-line of bluffs where outback
and ocean collide, two deserts, rock
to reef; knew rain

as reluctant manna. (I know Noble
Savagery is bogus —
I *like* my wires, my digital sonatas,
laptop and remote. But in the rubble

of her failing words something
of me too lies unaddressed. Song

by song, cell by cell, the dying
take galaxies along

with them into the grave — or
should. She does. Any death,
I used to feel, has to cancel a star
from the canopy, and with

all its satellites; but what of me, us,
this manic, fractured consciousness?
This at least we should have
the right to know before we leave,

that dying we deprive the world
of something whole. What is it I killed
that gnaws me now? What did you wall
away still murmuring? Fallout, ash in the well;

I know a desert when I'm in one.) Soon
her eyes will pool with the ceiling's
grey pasteboard overcast, the uncoilings
of soul into circuitry done,

and now for eulogy what I need
most is to goad my*self*, soul
corroded by years of trivial
discourse, data, to praise — a shade

re-fleshing body and senses through
spells of deep song: this tongue too
is a moment of moistened dust, of breath,
and each death's a fierce urging, though

hers most of all: a death within a death.

ENGLISH CEMETERY, GASPÉSIE

In a corner of the yard, quiet
And discreetly removed from worn, grey-
Shouldered monuments, you find the least
Ancient headstones weathering uneasily
On the lip of a seacliff. Giving onto the gulf
And east winds, these smaller markers glow
White as sails in the sun's offing; lean in the gust
Like fishermen over a deck's edge. On the brink
Of a shrinking headland, stripped willows
Hunch and quaver.
                    Even the clearest of the stones
Seem to list into whispering
Sallow earth, *Sacred*
To the Heart of Susannah Jane Tom Sommers
is laid here, and John Francis Mahon, who
Died on the Magdalen River 1910 and left
no one behind
                (except
perhaps the inscriber —)

Other stones are not so easy to read.
Only seventy years have sanded them,
salted them white until
now in the annulling sunlight
they are wholly illegible — runes
in an abandoned tongue,
ideas on a blank slate —

but someone must have carved them
once, cracked them in stone
with strong hands and Anglican assurance believing

they would endure for centuries

The yard however is empty at my visit —
no English speakers live
so far east now
their last words engraved years ago

                     And lying among them somewhere
the scribe, a nameless sexton
who did double-duty with chisel and spade
the last of his enclave
to die perhaps
wondering in the end
who would keep the lawn trimmed
who polish and clean the stones

aware at his last sigh
of a mute wind
hammering the walls

GRAVESONG

Jan. 02

It's said that the dead want us worthy of something.
Why do you wait till the waiting fills years?
Pain shovelled deep has no chance to bloom open.
A grave, a stringless guitar, a lost song.

Enough. They must hate to see us here sleeping.
Why will you stall till the stalling's your life?
It's wake yourself now or never be woken.
Lifetimes you waited for the right phone to ring.

The drowned, it was said, could be heard at night singing.
Why do you never set out while you can?
It's fix yourself now or always be broken.
A grave, a stringless guitar, a last song.

BLACKJACK

Hit: to take another card, and risk breaking.
Stand: to stick with what you have.

The dealer is dailiness, and the asking —
hit or stand? — comes more often than you guess.
Missed cues can fill a life. Or you signal wrong,

the house responds, no recourse. Standing with less
may be safer — you know the odds — but even then
the temptation is to hit. Sometimes loss

at long odds looks better than a sure win;
as if winning were a sure thing, ever.
In some dreams a familiar house will open

into unsuspected rooms, door after door
glides ajar, yet you hang back and consciousness
cuts in like an eviction. But what if you were

not so anxious to wake back into your less
uncharted life, and chanced those farther rooms . . . ?
Caution cancels love's richer part; eros,

sequestered in home safety, always seems
to die by inches. The house wins by turning
its people into furniture. Many tombs

are made of unplayed cards. It's me I'm warning
here. Hit when the asking happens. The house
may have its system, but you're not through learning.

THE PEACE OF HIGH PLACES

Her map shows the bottomlands where deer drink rain,
the dredge-ponds healed over by slow
films of time-lapse ice,
and sad, seasonal bungalows
on the ridge-rim of town, closed down
for winter, pipes drained,
beds cold —

Among juniper and stripped willow scrub
cranberries spring from cheechako graves
in the still chillness so beloved by hunters
and also by their game.

The lost sun has left its light in the fruit
and the eye in love always seeks in the heathery
groundcover mossed removes where any two
might lie together, somehow.

Her map shows the bottomlands where
deer drink rain, cupped in leaf-loam
or hollowed lobes of granite,
and a fleeting refuge
on the city's ridge-rim, closed down
for winter, pipes drained,
bed cold.

THE SHADOW BOXERS

Each year more of your life lost to shadow.
Small hours, blown open, blare with the soundtrack
of your hindsight, faces framed in the Prado
of memory seem realer than your son's, wisecracks
of an ex-ex-something outstabbing the actual
damage of sprain or wound. So it starts again,
night's neural colloquy, the patient quarrel
exhumed, ex-rival you again cross-examine

and now it's you there in the dock as the court's
night-attorney mocks all your explanatory
gab (what you really meant, what you worry
she heard) — you and all sworn desperadoes
of the backward glance: self-held prisoners
in the mind's shrinking cell, battling shadows.

THE MOVER

(Valerio Magrelli, 1992)

> *'What is translation?' On a platter*
> *the pale, flaming head of a poet.*
> — Nabokov

The mover who means to
clean out my room is doing
the same job as me. I
too move something — words —
to a new building, words
not mine, setting hands to things
I don't quite know, not quite
comprehending what I move.
Myself I move — translate
pasts to presents, to presence, that
travels sealed up, packed in pages, or
within crates bearing the inscription
FRAGILE. Don't know what's in them. And
this is what the future holds —
this shuttling, the metaphor, the tense
and manual grammar,
the transfer, the figure
of speech, the moving-
company come to move you.

LIKE A MAN

(Catullus, c. 65 BCE)

Enough of this useless moping, Catullus,
it's over, write it off. Back then
when she was yours, the sun always shone
and you were on her like the sun,
insatiable, as she was, and she'll
never have it so good again.
Always at her heels, her side, or
inside her, Catullus, and that was
fine, whatever you wanted she wanted
and the sun — there's no denying it —
always shone.

        Now she's changed, gone cold,
and you'll have to be the same —
not pitiful, like this, no whiner, idler,
sorry stalker, tavern fixture.
Take it like a man. So here's so long.
When Catullus makes up his mind, girl,
that's it. He won't come haunting
your doorway, nights, like love's hunched
beggar . . . but then again, who will?
Your nights will be as cold as his!
How will that suit you for a life?
Who'll come to see you then? Who
flatter you on your looks, give you
what he gave you all the time, and
take you around, kiss you,
be your fan? And you, girl —

who are *you* going to kiss,
yes, and bite . . . ?

                       Ah, Catullus,
enough, you know it's over.
And you're taking it like a man.

THE SLEEP AT SEA

(Homer, The Odyssey, Book 13, lines 76-93)

Now the crewmen sit to their oars in order and slip
the cable from the bollard hole and heave backwards
so their oarblades chop at the swell and churn up water
while over Odysseus sweet sleep irresistibly
falls so fathomless and sound it might almost be the sleep
of death itself. And the ship like a team of stallions
coursing to the crack of the lash with hoofs bounding
high and manes blown back like foam off the summits of waves
lunges along stern up and plunging as the riven
rollers close up crashing together in her wake
and she surges on so unrelenting not even a bird
quick as the falcon could have stayed abreast . . .
So she leaps on splitting the black combers bearing
a man godlike in his wisdom who has suffered years
of sorrow and turmoil until his heart grew weary
of scything a path home through his enemies or the furious
ocean; but now he sleeps profoundly, with all his griefs,
asleep at his side, forgotten.

PATIENT FRAME (2010)

It is very strange that the years teach us patience; that the shorter our time,
the greater our capacity for waiting.

— Elizabeth Taylor

Somewhere in the distance
You and I had fought the monster to a draw.

— Paul Siebel

Monstrous acts are fundamentally impatient.

— Stamátis Smýrlis

HOME MOVIES, 8 mm

What holds you here, besides small shocks
of delight, then embarrassment, seeing these too-fast
films unravelling, mute but for the sprockets'
plastic chatter, an outboard roar as the almost

antique projector, Yashica 1965, splashes clips
of faces in their once-loved form (forgotten
till now — interred in the nerves) on screen. What keeps
you here, tensed, if not frustration

at your impotence to intervene — reach back
and brace the hand holding the camera that pans
away, yet again, with a young hand's
impatience to contain all: slaphammer first home, a block

of Main Street rising between houses
to a mine's brontosaur headframe, in the laser-
blue noon of subarctic winter —
then, in a dress-coat the colour of roses,

a mother, breaking the frame, waving a newsreel's
sped-up wave, while from the left a dog lollops in,
unrecalled as ever so small,
so awkward! — and you rush the screen,

kneel closer and again the camera
swivels away —
stout neighbour in dark overcoat and fedora,
mouth going — while to the left you can almost *see*

her and that dog in the dark, or wherever the place
is, forty years out of frame (both dead now), as the man in the coat
tips his hat and the scene cuts, to white. Greece
then, Nipissing, faces in flashes, the light

sallowed, even children stained by that ambery
tone, as the lens pivots faster, refuses focus,
close-up, the patient frame. I know how memory —
what these reels were meant to fortress —

aims the same fickle lens, leaving gaps and blurs
in the record, but what of the eye itself, as it glides
over a lifetime's loves the same way, careless
and rushed, a manic amateur,

and the little reel clicks down inside?

If I could start over, I would stare and stare.

SELECTED MONSTERS

for Barbara Gowdy

In Florence, circa 1460, Cosimo de' Medici enclosed a mixed group of animals in a
pen and invited Pope Pius II to attend the spectacle, which was meant to determine
which beast was the most ferocious: the lion, the fighting bull, the bloodhound, the
gorilla, or perhaps the giraffe — an animal then known in Europe as a Camelopard.

"Holiness, with these monsters in close quarters
we're sure to have a brawl." But the new Caesars
lacked some Roman secret — razors

in the stable straw, or a bonus
bout of starvation, glass goads in the anus
or a goon squad of trainers

who knew how to crack a good whip.
So this static, comic crèche — this flop —
a Peaceable Kingdom with cud-chewing bull, ape

absently wanking, lion asleep, bloodhound's
limbs twitching in some wet dream of a hind's
stotting fetlocks, and the giraffe, free of wounds,

hunched by the fence, its trembling yellow ass
not enough to coax an assault. Pius
cleared his throat. "The Florence heat, I suppose,"

he yawned. "I've seen sportier feats
at a Synod. When's dinner?" Trailing hoots
and loutcalls, the mob drained out at the exits,

the boxseats emptied, the media crews
taxied elsewhere, till finally Cosimo's
bloodpit was a high-shelved archive of human refuse —

handbills, tickets, peanut shells, all set to motion
by a new wind, as if performing for that pen
of blinking inmates, who remained there . . . still remain

in the blinding empirical lens of the sun
and uranium rainfall, centuries on.
                              "At eight.
Expect exotic cuts. And excellent wine."

LIFE!

after Míltos Sachtoúris

Night in the all-night
drug mart
where a kneeling
horse
devours
the vinyl tile
and a woman
with curious vernal burns
is being treated
urgently
while the
ghost despairingly
weeps
by the magazines

YOU KNOW WHO YOU ARE

While my friend (the kid
you misconducted — the boy you left
songless in a sexton's yard among the open
doors of dug graves, among which he passed
the rest of a life curtailed, half-
cursed) coughed
and edged toward his solo
consummation, sir, you did zero
but soil other choirboys in your charge, and coyly
charm, flirt with the mothers, eventually
passing some pensive months in minimum —
society claiming its pound of flesh, to quote
just one of your hack apologists (the boy
himself is now an ounce of dust) —
where, I ungraciously suppose, you must
have checked your mirrored face, to rehearse the miens
of remorse, that sanctimonious sideshow,
along with other states of which your choir used to descant
in the superb manner you, a fine teacher, taught well: *repent*,
for example, or *atone*,
which to you must have sounded too much like *alone*
(a place where you're saddled with your own soul
and nobody there to perform for, fool
or abuse). Hard time! Tonight, sir, I still accuse
you, who — while earth slowly unstrings a boy
in his *lento* measure of staved ground —
still savours the tang
of August tomatoes, chords of Fauré's *Requiem*
(two years served, in fairway minimum)
and the rectifying esteem of upstanding Ang-
lican pals. So in your pool or Jacuzzi

wallow pink as a gangster, as water
bubbles like laughter, or the last
cantique of boy sopranos
vanished into their lives — bass now, tenor —
or through some colder
one way door.

CONSTANCE & HER STALKERS

In the end, sometimes, starvation simply arrests the heart.

— Jean Takamura, *Hungers*

Useless, useless,
*   sign the hands of the assassin*
*   hunted down in the straw.*

Or the searchteam's
*   pilot in the typhoon*
*   forgetting his horizon.*

Useless the locks on
*   windows, doors.*
*   Helpless the law.*

Constance was always on the cusp
of something crazy, her windows, doors
unlocked while a casual
strangler cased the trailer parks
and dirt lanes fringing Reno.

We warned her, but she was starving
and it sapped her concentration.

Wish you lived in the world sometimes,
I told her, foraging in the minus hours
through her phantom pantry,
empty. James Brown steaming in stereo;
neat Tanqueray. She said,
We can do dark

another day, nothing ever
has to be relived.

Under adobe
listening to the desert
wind's weird tunings, remote
wasping of a pilot, miles higher,
surveillant — maybe an eye
on the man in the news,
that failed assassin and
feared (by the sane)
assailant.

> *She said she was surviving*
> *but there was talk of an operation.*

To what were you constant?
Your hunger. Lurid maroon
tattoo of forearm scars,
that wreck in progress.

Sincere nihilist.

I saw myself complacent, un-
grateful for all earth had given.

That night, the strangler again
struck the outskirts, again
failing, just, to kill, but laying down
further strata of fear.
The reason why I'm here.
Near dawn I ran home
down a scorpion turnpike

and a squadcar slowed and coasted
beside me, the face in there probing,
the beacon's coronary strobing
lighting a broken arc
of the desert floor ——

SOME OTHER JUST ONES

A footnote to Borges

The printer who sets this page with skill, though he may not admire it.
Singers of solo expertise who defer and find harmonies instead.
Anyone whose skeleton is susceptible to music.
She who, having loved a book or record, instantly passes it on.
Whose heart leans into a reach of vacant road, the fervent surge of acceleration,
    psalm of the tires.
Adults content to let children bury them in sand or leaves.
Those for whom sustaining hatred is a difficulty.
Surprised by tenderness on meeting, at a reunion, the persecutors of their youth.
Likely to forget debts owed them but never a debt they owe.
Apt to read Plutarch or Thich Naht Hahn with the urgency of one reading the
    morning news.
Frightened ones who fight to keep fear from keeping them from life.
The barber who, no matter how long the line, will not rush the masterful shave
    or cut.
The small-scale makers of precious obscurios—pomegranate spoons, conductors'
    batons, harpsichord tuning hammers, War of 1812 re-enactors' ramrods,
    hand-cranks for hurdy-gurdies.
The gradeschool that renewed the brownfields back of the A & P and made them
    ample miraculous May and June.
The streetgang that casts no comment as they thin out to let Bob the barking
    man squawk past them on the sidewalk.
The two African medical students in Belgrade, 1983, who seeing a traveller lost
    and broke took him in and fed him rice and beans cooked over a camp
    stove in their cubicle of a room and let him sleep there while one of them
    studied all night at the desk between the beds with the lamp swung low.
Those who sit on front porches, not in fenced privacy, in the erotic inaugural
    summer night steam.
Who redeem from neglect a gorgeous, long-orphaned word.

Who treat dogs with a sincere and comical diplomacy.
Attempt to craft a decent wine in a desperate climate.
Clip the chain of consequence by letting others have the last word.
Master the banjo.
Are operatically loud in love.
These people, without knowing it, are saving the world.

THINGS

(Jorge Luis Borges)

This cane, loose change, my ring of keys,
this trusty lock, belated notes which the short
time left to me will leave no time to peruse,
the deck of cards and the checkerboard,
a book, and in its pages a shrivelled flower,
memento of an afternoon that was surely
unforgettable (forgotten now, however) —
this west-facing mirror, violet with the fiery
show of an illusory dawn. How many things —
doorsills, doornails, mapbooks, wineglasses, tongs —
slave their lives away in our service, taciturn,
unseeing, so inscrutably reserved . . .
they will endure beyond our own going
and they will never realize we are gone.

OUTRAM LAKE

Lake buried under the Hope Slide, Hope, B.C., January 1965

The rhyme of your death revives the couplet.

No one's with you on the porch the bitter night
  you submit yourself to winter, to wed,
    with ice, your absence
to a buried wife's, dying toward her
  in a way that's anaesthetic
    and yet, in its simple dignity, aesthetic too —
that would matter to you —
  while in the vital, summerlike hum
    of sodium streetlamps, a cold confetti of snowflakes
settles homeward, marking this reunion, till it's time
  and timeless, the lush numbness of freezing
    stills you, and your lips and fingers
are done versing.

      A cold spring
and we drive from the coast into the Cascades
to witness how a body of water can vanish:
                  this prior loss
could hardly have rhymed less — deafening,
fast — massed panzers of boulders and snow
loosed downvalley over a doomed throughway
to plough traffic under, then bombarding
onward to bury Outram Lake, ages
deep, under a jumbled slag
like dense, enigmatic wording.

(wait for me   in that winter room —)

Different, yet here too a beauty
interred, flow stalled (we thought at first),
until, miles downvalley, reading in the car,
we came to ourselves along a glacial stream
braiding green with subconscious silts
from under time's not quite decisive slide —

Richard Outram, poet, died Port Hope, 21 January 2005

TWO TANKAS

(Onakatomi Yoshinobu, c. 950)

1

The lone doe that lives
among the mountains of pine
where no leaves fall
can know the autumn has come
by her own cry alone.

2

The guardfires that burn
at the imperial gate —
embering all day
and then, at nightfall, flaring —
such is the love that glows in me.

JETLAG

June, Arkhangel'sk

It's night in your bones   though noon. A no one
room, drugged with sunlight of a skewed
latitude,
the fizz in capillaries behind the eyes' red rind, un-

housed, stalling hydraulics of the heart. The insomniac
lens of the sun deepens this lag, and   dizzies, is dis-
inclined to set, reset this
body clock,

wonky, jarred as a man who bends to rinse
his face clean of a night's journey and straightens
to meet himself above the sink: no mirror, his face
drywall. Such times a phantom tourist

might urge to mind moments that lodge you
deep in a life:
                    when you first heard last century's best tenor,
Jussi Bjoerling, skewer the skynote in "O Helga Natt," and swore
no more lies and of course still lied but less and less as years
went and years went and that high C went on
compounding in your soul, or
                    for the first time kissed her breasts in the fire-alley
of a mountain town, under the startled brainwaves
of the aurora borealis
                    or hiked the low cliffs of Naxos with the child
on your back, her weight bracing your step to soil
so at last you felt present — sheathed in sheer being —
she chanting the genesis of all she spied,

lending back through the ear's narrowed estuary
that urgent inventory . . .

these things you summon to seeing, to rudder you
in the real   in a no one room
with night in your bones ——

HERSELF, REVISED

There's a final bedtime when the father reads
to his daughter under the half-moon lamp.
The wolf-eyed dog sits guard on the snowy
quilt at their feet — ears pricked, head upright
like a dragon on its hoard — while the daughter's
new clock ticks on the dresser. When the father
shuts the book, neither feels in the cool sigh
cast from its pages a breath of the end —
and how can it be that this ritual
will not recur? True, this latest story
is over, *Treasure Island,* which held them
a dozen nights, but "the end" has arrived
this way often before. Maybe she's tired
of the rite, or waking to a sense of herself
revised? Maybe he's temporarily bored,
or unmoored, reading by duty or rote,
turning deeper inside his own concerns.

How does the end enter? There's a hinging
like a book's sewn spine in the raw matter
of time — that coded text, illegible —
and stretched too far, it goes. An innocent
break, the father off one weekend or the child
sleeping at a friend's, followed by a night
or two she wants to read alone, or write,
for a change, in her new padlock journal.
She has no idea what has changed. She
can't know that the enlargement of her life
demands small death after death, and this one,
the latest, is far from last. She will not
notice this death, being so intent on life —

so implied in its stretching crewelwork
of seconds.
           Some nights later, suddenly,
writing cheques or checking email, he might
notice and wonder at the change. In a sense
such minor passings pre-enact his own.
For a moment he might lay down his pen,
forget the figures, peer over the roofline
and find she was right — Orion, rising,
is more blueprint of butterfly, or bird,
than hunter. How does it enter, through what rift
or flaw? Maybe it doesn't enter at all.
It was there in every sentence: the end.

THE LAST READER

The woman whose eyesight is fading tries to read
her son's first book. It's long, 300 pages,
and she can take in a page a night, at best.
When the doctor says she has less than a year

it's not her eyesight he means. As she reads, death
gets on with its own cunning work — studying,
mastering the subtle codes, transcribing her
cell by syllable into the vast anthology

of the dead. Death never doubts itself, as her son,
she knows, must do. Death gets it right each time.
She reads till all sense stops rising from the page,

this plot no lamp enlightens. A week's worth left
to be unveiled. In the still-encrypted world
she and her son the last reader and writer.

ON A CHANGE OF ADDRESS CARD SENT A FEW WEEKS BEFORE YOU DIED

I suppose, Aunt Bette, you will have sent
many like this: the NEW ADDRESS you list, almost
illegibly, is one you just passed through, en route
to a lasting address. Like most of the stressed

people who fill out these chits, Aunt
Bette, you leave the OLD ADDRESS slot
blank, presumably the recipient
already knows that one, and if not

why would they need it now? No one
needs it now. It's just this sort of official
redundancy you'd always impatiently shun —
or so I guess, not having known you well

enough, while knowing you each year of my life,
since I grew aware I had a life, you letting us
loaf at your bar like grownups, safe
from the hypothermic surf we'd just

"survived" (a sister and I in the shallows
of Trout Lake), as you boiled slabs of Baker's
Chocolate in milk, Maria Callas
shrilling from the hi-fi, to make us

hot drinks; chain-smoking, raucous
with laughter, grilling orange
cheddar sandwiches on rye; you with grievous
bruises under the eyes, strange

badges to me then (seeming to fit the word
widow), though at some point I heard of
your "epic insomnia" — another chord
between our lives, like the love

for Pushkin you passed to me, and Robeson,
and the dreamtime deserts of the Centre,
where at nineteen I would wander
with a pack, never seeing the reason

(obvious, now) I'd chosen *there* was what I
heard at the bar — of the Martian-
red plains of Nullarbor, salt lakes of Kiti,
legends of the Bunyip, the Southern Ocean.

Ignorance of what formed and cast oneself
across worlds is a kind of freedom, no doubt,
but to saunter inside myths of Self-
making is just life without gratitude

or form. In those free seasons I liked to pretend
I'd no address, no author. Now I seem to yearn
to fill out a form, backdated to then —
your name (and others). Last time we went:

"I think I'm ready for something a bit more
permanent," you said, winking, even then en route
to this culminating locale, where your
husband has long been established, Bette,

and I've come to see you, dwelling now
not far from my mother, under flower-

red chestnuts that, as a child, you never knew
down under, while stars with names you never

did quite learn now bloom, perennial, above.
SPEERS, BEECHWOOD, Chestnut Lane,
Row Number 17,
Plot 5.

KID BROTHER, BLACK OCTOBER

You could have danced more and filled fewer spreadsheets,
feared time less — not cordoned yourself in these clock-
quartz cells with the blind broker, whose costive thoughts
log overtime and follow the Dow (and lesser sites)
where even the parasites have parasites.
Don't buy into this futures
                                        "paradise,"
all the time there is is here, and skeptics too
sometimes recant, return to life in the current.

If your malaise isn't viral, why does it keep vectoring
south like an avian plague? I protest the repealed siestas
of Rhodes, Rome, and Oaxaca — all that olive-
scented slumber and shuttered ecstasy, lost —
                                        little skinflint —
don't go back to your screen, we've a flat-top guitar
and medicinal rye. Your soul may be a hoarder's gated hovel
but I love you, even spent. Skeptics, too, sometimes repent,
return to song in the timeless.

MEMO TO A SELF

Nothing fills the famished chasm. Drape its walls with degrees,
blue ribbons, ego's little
luxury supplies —
cram it with Chairs of this or that, titles,

money — or, if not, then surely love? Of a lifetime
friend? Still no,
not quite. A husband — wife?
Or child, that love lacking fine print or proviso?

For all it should, not yet. Zero fills the famished chasm.
Say as much, then go down inside
and sit there a time. It's a womb
in form, but this time in you, and so far barren. Be quiet. Reside

nowhere else for hard trimesters. If the space is dry, replenish it with
the amniotic brine of tears
long due, then learn to breathe
the green element beyond speech, as ego sputters, slowly tires

and drowns, and something else of you
readies for the immense and wave-like
labour that remains.

RUN WITH HER

He was tired, the gloss
had gone off the day,
but there was still the dog,
pacing, appearing at his desk
in indicting silence, with that chafing
yet stoical stare — the dog drawing him
on and out into day's dimming aftermath, earth
turning its face from the sun's latest extinction
as he and the dog plod, side by side, out of the city
into cityless time — the reliquary forest still cached
with ancestral smells, where the reviving man and
would-be wolf (loping ahead, nose low, feverishly
truffling the cedar duff) truly run now, as if hounding more
than phobic voles, squirrels and the gone worlds hunkered
in either mind, like the first hunter and wolf to run in squadron,
before any farm or village, mill, metropolis or bylaw—all the
sensible taming and setting-to-good-use, those leashes
we're linked to, our PIN-tinkling collars and other losses
and gains. Yet for now all losses lag behind him
and the dog with her panting grin, full gallop, his pulse
pacing hard, fired up, keeping stride — deeper
into stands of pine and the great, sky-
rooted oaks, along fading, finally
untakable trails, her tail (as he
slows now, stumps in pursuit)
almost lost, a hinge of smoke
in the gloom, receding
ahead into the past —

.

SKY BURIAL, THE SCHOLAR

In that dream, scavengers
bore his skeleton into the sky
piecemeal,

disarticulate and silenced, save
for the sighs of the ventriloquist
wind in hollowed ulna,

susurrations in the radius,
a femoral music, a marrow
of music — and he no more

than those tunnelling tunes, Self
and the elements
unsundered at last, skull's oubliette

unlocked, cracked
like the clamshell a kittiwake
lets fall over rocks ——

and this is the eventual
ecstasy of skeptics ——
those who swapped the rush of being

in earth's brief, arduous eden
for bunkered years in solitary,
imposing self-sentence

sentence by sentence,
who loved things only
aslant, never with the heart

full-frontal, who never once
forgot their own names when sea-
or skinscapes intervened,

never saw (eyes lasered
clear of the cataracts
of habit) rain falling

like a ransom, the stars
stammering celestial news
and the old moon, reminted.

A MONSOON SUICIDE

after gestures by Weldon Kees & Edvard Munch

In this hired room, my window
gives onto shredded sea, intruding

slats between stanzas of foam,
those long lines of breakers, scrolling

slowly into noise. The window's sealed
to cut the roar, but the woman who came

with the room has brought the sea
within (her salt, her soft, nautical snores),

while out there the plying and replying
surf goes on erasing the littoral, the break-

water barely holding. Some dreams drift me
outward like a liminal form

into winds that are deafening the shore
and land: a note of departure I've been

nearing from the first, by instalment
like the tides, at a leased window, giving

onto perpetuity. *Do I miss the earth?* If she
woke, we might speak. Let in the storm.

I will. For fear this sill will rust and freeze,
lips locked after the words are done.

                              Crack
through the spaces lean out and scream ——

LOVE SONNET XVII

(Pablo Neruda)

I love you not as if you were topaz, a saline
rose, quiverful of carnations strewing flame —
I love you in secrecy, as one loves certain
unclear things, between shadow and the soul. No bloom

on the plant I love as I love you, which retains,
interred in itself, the light of its lost blossoms,
while in my flesh the dense, ascending fragrance
earth generates now darkly resides, by reason

of your love. I love you without knowing how, when,
where from, I love you straight on, no complication
or pride, love you like this because I've never known

another way to love: *you* and *I* have no more meaning,
so close that your hand on my body is my own,
so close now your eyelids close with my sleeping.

WORLD ENOUGH

A ruckus
of ravens
disbands
over the nuisance grounds

where every trace
of us two (save
what the grave
grabs) ends up —

everything is
rental, everything
is lent, ex-
piring, the thrilling

Jag, liver-
spotted, lichened
with rust,
the dream house

passing through these
hands to ex-
ecutors, like our lease-
to-lose

allotment of carbon
moving on
as it must
(even dust

falls to dust).
We own so little
of ourselves, how
did we think to own

anything of the world?
A momentary estate —
and yet, for all that,
all things here,

even the dumpsite
and the creosote
ravens, seem this sunrise
startled into being, coined

and kenned
to newness,
in chorus with chaos,
this ruckus of birds

centrifugal
as red-shifted stars
in a cosmos
unfinished unfolding.

THE WAKING COMES LATE (2016)

The basic subject of poets is their own living body.

— Giórgos Seféris

Nor shall I care to write poetry that is not praise,
lamentation, or both.

— Stamátis Smýrlis

INSPIRED BY A LINE BY PAUL CELAN

Betrink dich und nenn sie Paris

Each day I wake feeling I've already failed.
Tonight let's get wrecked and call it Venice.
A woman I loved lied that she was healed
and for a night until waking, we were. I was born
with a mortgage, now show me the house, the home,
slip me the dose that'll make me care less. I wake
each day feeling I've already torn
what I meant to rethread. (Did anything seem
in Eden, or was it all its own is?)

There was that woman, so enlisted in life,
one of passion's true recruits, *Love*, I said,
I am so bad at loving, and the usual biz
ensued — scenes, loss and its isotopic
slow-fade, never done. On the deathbed of the skeptic
where he slept each night of his dying life
he said, *It was hard having so little skin-to-skin*
with the world—but look on my works!
                                        Venice
is sinking, and it might be the case
it was never the key at all. Said a small voice
in the cirrus of a dream, *Love is its own abode.*
Not sure what it meant, though I think I knew once.
There is some cold road that you must renounce.

THE LAST STURGEON

Deltawave shadows
of his deeds
and didn'ts, slid
under his shoes
like fillet knives, severing
soles from soil,
so he always walked
a little above his life,
not knowing it was
his life, while it waned
from waking-coma
to coma.
          Came a land-
locked night
he dreamed that he'd
landed the last sturgeon in the world
and she looked bad —
shrunken, bludgeoned,
a blue-ribbed CAT scan
of herself, her buckled
gills gawping,
a foam of green roe
welling from her mouth.

Each egg
was a tear, a tiny, entreating
vowel he couldn't quite hear
as he cast round the boat (now morphing
into a mountain shack)
for *water*, the merest
rainpool, or glacial stream,

he panicked,
my dearest,
my loved one,
let me bear you back
to haven — by river
the ocean
is never far.

VARIATIONS ON A CRANIAL CAT SCAN PROFILE
AFTER A LARYNGEAL FRACTURE

Most intimate
of portraits, yet
clinically impersonal,

like a medschool textbook
graphic — cross-section
of a cadaver's

head and throat — or
a silhouette embossed
on a dime or quarter,

the chilling silver
of some undead realm.
You cannot love this monster —

the werewolf rictus
of grated teeth, the side-seen eye's
great, avid globe;

periscope esophagus, probing
up through the contused throat
as if to peer out

through the silenced mouth.
*You might never speak again
in more than this rustle.* So what

good now (wonders
the locked-in frontal lobe)
is this lobe, encased

in its hyperbolic brow,
the bloated cartoon
thought bubble

of consciousness. What use
if it can't express, explain
itself naked (save to itself)

or in thin, cold cuneiform
as on this page,
two or more bone-shores

from life? So now, in the husk
of the broken voice-box,
see it mass on the scan

with that swelling — a welling
abscess of all you failed
to say, and might not now,

and the pressure collects
until you long to lean
an ear next to the lips of this

ghoul onscreen — to midwife words
if they strain half-free —
I meant to tell you, I

thought I told you, I couldn't
quite, but open, stay, God
help you if,

even now, you won't bear
into being, on a breath,
something

more than mere —

AFTER THE CAT SCAN

Larynx shattered in a crash and the doctor
orders you to gag it: "Pen and pad, pal — write
what you need to say." So you bronchiate
goodbye to your wife and daughter
and pack for the cabin at Desert Lake,
mute's retreat now, where you'll nod from the dock
at dawn-drunk anglers (bass, trout, and walleye),
who deem your pantomime thoughtful, fish-friendly.
Bit lonely in lack of the dog, who so loves
to boat in beside you, lunge onto the dock
as you ship oars, then vanish for hours.
But without your clamor to collar her back . . .
Three a.m. — outside, naked, you re-inflame
your throat chiding woodchucks chewing the frame,
your "yells" like whispers of a Scorsese thug.
(A long lag before they deign to scatter.)
        It's like you're an ancient, dreaming you're defunct,
striving to holler home across the river
that lets no sound slip back, not to wife, daughter,
even the dog with her large-array ears
who's loyally listening, shores apart —
who'll be listening for your tone of praise
until the hour her last faculties fade
and she hears only, faintly, the boatman's oars
stroking toward her like a muted heart.

BAFFLED IN ASHDOD, BLIND IN GAZA

Eden Abergil: former Israel Defense Forces soldier who, in August 2010, posted photos of herself smiling beside bound and blindfolded Palestinian prisoners. She labeled her Facebook album, "The army . . . best time of my life."

Eden
Abergil,
Eden of Ashdod, you only did
what any young recruit might do —
what I might have done myself, a little scared, a little
stoned (on your own strength, Eden,
as if each beautiful bullet you packed
were a pill — designer hybrid
of Percocet and blow, to anneal you against all
that's frail and slow, that's bound,
beyond help) —
    And so these Facebook pics
and that bit of bad press (don't worry, Eden, the news —
save on Al Jazeera and in the tabloids of Tehran —
has already moved on).
    You don't get it. You protest. Your little shoot
killed no one! So then, why are the great Jews —
the poets and performers, the scientists, inventors,
philosophers, reformers — those truest
People of the Book — all weeping quietly
in their tombs: Paul Celan,
Hannah Arendt, almond-bitter Mandel-
stam, Marx and Einstein, all of them sad
insomniacs of the hinterlife, tallowing
hours away in the earth
to understand this "Facebook," as well as the smirk
this now-world wears: failed future that won't leave them to sleep,

not even the adamant suicides — Benjamin, Levi, Celan—
especially not the suicides.

And you sit baffled in Ashdod, Eden,
wondering why nobody caught the joke;
meantime the army's marketing folks
Photoshop your face to a blur, but

too late, you're famous! Your poses
pathogenic, spreading via tweets and texts, and sickening . . .

sickening no one at all — we've all gone immune — all
but the hopeful dead, though of course
they're dead and can't die again
of our indignities.

Eden,
Eden of ash, your grand-
parents were the Nazi War — Eden
of Ashdod, *der Tod*
is still in the story, the frontier
between millennia didn't keep it out,
the Human Future didn't phase it out,
now it's posted, grinning, on your wall.

Let every wall wail.

LENINGRAD

(Osip Mandelstam, 1930)

I returned to my city familiar as tears,
as my pulse, as boyhood's swollen glands.
So quickly drink down, now that you're here,
the cod liver oil of these riverside lamps

and recognize instantly December's brief day,
where egg yolk mingles with ominous tar.
Petersburg, I'm not yet ready to die!
My telephone numbers remain in your care;

Petersburg, I have an address list still
to help me track down the voices of the dead.
I live on a black staircase, and the bell

wrenched out with its veins hits me on the temple.
Rattling the door-chains as if they were shackles
I wait through the night for the cherished guests.

THE CITY

(Konstantínos Kaváfis, 1910)

You said, "I will go to another country, another shore,
find a distant city better than my own.
All I attempt here is destined to ruin
and my heart, like a corpse, lies buried.
How long will my mind here mark time, wearied,
decayed? Wherever I turn, wherever I gaze:
the black debris of my life in this place
where I killed so much time: years squandered and soured."

You will find no other country, no other shore —
the city will follow you. You will wander the same
streets and enclaves, aging, in these self-same
rooms fading slowly to pale. Your escape will end
every time in this place. Don't hope for some other land —
there's no ship out for you, no road away. As you've wasted
your life here, in this small corner, you've destroyed it
everywhere else in the world.

WHEAT TOWN BEER LEAGUER, GOOD SNAPSHOT, NO BACKHAND

Sometimes gladly I would skate away
from the simian prattle in my prefrontal lobe,
the desolate sierra of Mandatory Reads,
the whole envious exercise of Public Lit.

Then I see myself with you in some wind-burned
wheat town, raising cheerfully unsupervised kids,
you known locally for Odyssean dogwalks along the cedar windbreaks
through the poplared coulees, and me
playing third-line centre in a beer league — you in the bleachers
cheering wryly, me bleeding a little on the hashmarks
after conceding another collision to Weyburn's most
cruelly goateed defenceman.

And the compound stink of the arena — fabricated frost,
the popcorn stench of old hockey gloves — would flag
a curious liberty from the fakery
and fuckery of culture — its pretense that one is special, elect,
consecrated to a purer calling,
                                  when after all love
is the one calling of that kind, whoever hears it
and wherever, Yorkton
or the Latin Quarter, Medicine Hat or Venice.

(My slender, gentle mother, dead now ten years,
maybe it is simpler after all, happiness, goodness —
maybe you and Papa would have been as happy
in Kenora, or Cochenour, and sometimes
so gladly I would skate away —)

A COSMOS

In the wake of a month-long crimson tide,
as if the blighted sea were bleeding out,
phosphorescent plankton lapped the coastline, so every night
the caps of the great combers, luminescing
green in black waters, under a sky-tide of stars,
drew crowds down to Tragos Beach.

Third night somebody went in, and the father
followed with his daughter, fifteen, fearless,
their hands clasped in the caving breakers
buckling and torquing them under
as if to rip her free, her grip
loosening, her body in the sea aglow, looping
isotopic trails as she fought the undertow
in terrified delight, shrieking, swept back
into childhood, yet outbound as well
toward a life to come.
                As they broke
surface — sequined against the dark
by countless quanta of light — she seemed no mere
constellation but a cosmos, and even he
with his landlocked heart was portalled back
to earlier joys, and seas, yet by the same swell
cast outward, years beyond the coastal
shelf of the familial, to a solo
unmooring: all ties, all selves.

They waded back through blood-warm shallows
and up the beach, the tracks they left
aligned, aglow, and fading.

¡EVITE QUE SUS NIÑOS . . .!

1

On the shrink-wrapped shoreline a mourner
sits shiva for the seas, lapis
and lapping the last
living coast
with cesium.
So this is what a prayer is for.

2

Too late, I guess,
we learn what to love.
By the time I fell in love
with the planet
                    (a man was sighing
in the hypnagogic reefs of a dream)
it was dying.

3

And this just in,
approximated

from a near-extinct
lexicon

in a time of lethal
beachings —

                    the blue whales

                        bellow

                        below

UNTITLED

(Paul Celan)

What was written caves in,
what was spoken, seagreen,
flames in the bays,

among the molten names
the porpoises race,

here, in the eternal nowhere,
in memory of the over-
knelling bells in — (but where?) —

who
in this
shadow-quarter
is gasping, who
from beneath it
shimmers up, shimmers up, shimmers up?

COLLISION

Away in the eyefar
nightrise over the sapwood, and one likes
under hooves the heatfeel after sun flees, heat stays on this
smooth to the hoof hardpan, part trail
part saltlick now as snowlast moults back
into the sapwood
to yard and rot
and one sees moonrise mounding
over a groundswell, but too soon and swifter
like never the moon one knows, no moon at all,
two moons fawned, both small, too hot, they
come with a growling and
hold one fast, so chafing for flight
but what, what, what, what
wondering —

and one can't move and can't although one
knows from backdays, eared and glimpsed
through sapwood budwood cracklewood bonewood
flashes of this same Wolfing
                                    now upon one, still
stalls the hooves on the saltlick and the eyebright
creature squeals   afraid? — and one somehow
uphoofed in a bound not chosen high as if to flee with no
trying, no feeling, fallen   flankflat, fawnlike
eyes above in the eyefar closing small
with the world

                    and now from the stopped thing
comes what   its cub?   legged up on its hinds,
kneels low to touch, but in that awful
touch, no feel   no fear to feel
no at all ——

ALL RIVERS ARRIVE

She lays her cheek, slick with tears and snot,
on her mother's scarred and cooling chest, the breasts
years since removed, all flesh scraped bare
of the runged ribs beneath which now no stoic, solo
muscle knocks, and impossibly

a memory of milk returns —
the fleeting, timeless tenure of her suckling,
creamy sweet, yet salt as well, the feel
of life liquid in the mouth, now brimming
home to memory (if it be so),
                              as her own milk
once swelled her own breasts, she awaiting
the nurse who would bring her third child back,
the one they never brought back, so her breasts
seemed futile as the plastic sacs
hung here above a mother whose veins have ceased
to sip their saline,
                    each sac a clear
distended tear, the brine of her own tears
pooled on what remains of her mother's chest
as she — the child, returned — returns
that first life-gift of salt.

THE WEATHER ONLINE

Weather conditions current and overnight, temperature 9°C dropping after
midnight to 3°C. Chance of frost by dawn in low-lying areas. Winds northwest
20 gusting 35 km/hr. Barometric pressure 86 kilopascals and rising. Possibility
of scattered flurries.

The weather of other cities
signifies to new degrees
whenever she's away — each day you check and then check again
and wish you were there, or
wish you simply were
the wind, the cold, the snow that attends her — if in fact tonight
there's snow — or maybe the air
her face and chest will prow
at dawn as she steps out
onto Front or Shore. And searchlight spokes of morning sun
that fill her eyes you would like
to be as well, and so evoke
from the wells of each intended iris
hues not hers.
Has she layers enough? A polar front is pressing east
to frost the prairie stubble,
skeleton wheat towns
and ship-eating lakes,
and find her in Chicago, or Toronto,
by the lakeside, likely, her collar turned up (you turn her collar up)
and scarf tucked close
(you tuck her scarf in close
and once again consult
the weather online, *Conditions*
sunset, 6:08 p.m., unseasonally cold, skies clear, no moon).

UNTAKEN TURNS

Everyone kept talking about "the turn
in the poem," and it bothered the poet
that he couldn't see. Perhaps — the poet
thought — in his writing there was no such "turn,"
nor likewise in his life, which meant his road
was like a salt-flat dragstrip, he on it
pedal floored, no pensive pause or quiet
fork in the forest of midlife — no sane
tap of the brake and steering toward more
paced, and patient, tomorrows.
                                    Glare off the salt
had long since seared his peripheral vision,
he saw only ahead, he went only there
as on some grim, involuntary mission,
though his own poems, frantic, begged him Stop.

SONG OF THE GRAVES

(J. E. Villalta)

    For years in the dry ledger of nights and days
their bodies barely figured. Now the debt,
in an hour, is amortized, a moment arrives
when the lovers no longer own themselves
or even remember how they met
or where, on the island
        of Arawak graves.

    The bone-boats of the buried dead, becalmed
in loam, are now less lonelied,
while you two, the newer ones,
lie here among them,
        relimb and become them,
on the island of Arawak bones.

    Nothing will ever be virtual again,
it seems — such spells
leave more to keep than this cooling
imprint of bodies in leaves (soon covered, hidden,
like time-lapse graves) on a shoreline's
border uncertained by reeds:
        a line between whatever loves
and what once,
            on the island of Arawak graves.

TRAKL, 1913

To give to the truth what belongs to the truth ...

— Georg Trakl

The poet's grey hat, afloat on the lake, flags the place
where he marched himself under, his bowler
a buoy, last bubble on the waves
of the watery necropolis he might have dreamed up
the night before wading in —
gravefloats bobbing above the vertical dead,
a million floats, in files and rows,
over the weed-waving hair
of each head.
          Votive lilies and lacustral red
poppies flag where mourners oared past — mute
gondoliers with gifts — and on each float, epitaphic,
prescriptions in a stoned hand only Georg
(ex-druggist: now addict)
can grasp.
          From the shore, the others spy his hat!
Hollering they hurry down to restore him
from the green chloroform of the waters,
recruit him back to breathing,
enlist him back to life.

The war
the war
the war
has plans for Georg Trakl —
fate has filed fat dossiers of plans
for so many, soon
not even standing room

will remain in Middle Europe's
ancient lakes.

Now he coughs onto the sand
not blood but infant bile. *Smelling salts,
hot drinks: wake him back to this civilized dream.*

On the shore, a lipid spume like cream
on a field marshal's *Kaffee.*

And still the gentian current grieves
through the catacombs of Wolfgangsee.

CORONACH, POST-KANDAHAR

1

The damaged individual is invited to seek treatment,
albeit at some future date

Lance-corporal, here —
this comfort song, or (if prayer
is the protocol you prefer)
this prayer.

When you visit the clinic
we'll cook up a cure
for your sadness and panic.

Meanwhile pills,
meanwhile prayer.

Even to an atheist
God's the Omega
of a shotgun's business end.

2

The patient, still on a waiting list, suffers a major
coronary, for which he is promptly treated

His ribcage we cracked
and his heart we drew clear
like a red, writhing newborn
pulled from the rubble.

They said that in public
his punchlining brilliance
disguised desperation.

Take this, if you're manic —
come visit the clinic —
we've an opening
early next March.

Even to an atheist
God's the cold ordnance
of a twelve-gauge applied to the heart.

3

In which an appointment, of kinds, is finally found
for our patient

At the wake
(closed casket)

the piper
was drunk

but managed
a coronach.

MIKHALIÓS

(Kóstas Karyotákis, 1926)

Mikhaliós, they said, you're now a soldier.
Strutting, delighted, he set out with Vasílis
and Marís but he couldn't march, or shoulder
arms, or manage the simplest thing. "Master-
corporal," he was always murmuring, "Sir,
please let me go back to my village."

A year later, in hospital, he would stare
mutely through the window at the skies,
affixing a meek and nostalgic gaze
on some point beyond the horizon,
as if to find there someone to implore,
"Please, Sir, just let me go home."

But Mikhaliós died a soldier still.
His pallbearers were a handful of pals —
Marís, Vasílis, a few nameless others.
Above him they shovelled in the dirt,
though one bare foot they left sticking out —
poor boy, he was always a bit tall.

IN ORDER TO BURN

In a sleeping pill season, in a REM-stage remission,
revisit a curve in a certain cold river

where the birches are in full business
and the grass of the banks is wild mint.

It's years, yet you're both stretched out here still,
rib to rib, hearts happily talking over each other,

and above you somehow the same southerlies,
same sunfish school of pewter leaves

pulsing in ultramarine. Remembrance:
how every touch and utterance

seemed tender calamity, so even now,
in the locked-in stasis of this sedation,

the couple you made is still current
on that earth. You were conscious, then,

even sleeping, and what's wholly lived keeps looping
through some unforgetting amnion, so pulse

to pulse, fully personed, you return. (Not that she can —
yet see how, even now, she is nowhere else.)

THE MINOR CHORDS

build slowly, then linger. Think how the lone
sour note of some letdown, a little jab
or jilt, the kind that you'd work through soon

and forget, gets followed too closely
by the next, *We regret to inform you* (by email
or post), or some other fleeting, non-fatal snub —

then the clincher, the sharp or flat
that nails the chord, a lauded colleague's cocktail
froideur, or just a driver at a four-way

giving you the finger. So now again the minor
fall: you drag through days in a somber key,
like aftertones of a verdict murmured, you to you,

in the night. *Hey, loser.* Every failure
seems a small demise, a strange homecoming;
knowing it's not never helps. Brain gets wiser, gut

never gets it, stays a sucker too for the dulcet
jingles of praise, lucky runs, ribbons, raises,
as if fifty years of learning meant squat,

win or lose, captain or cut from the squad,
the limbic centre sends up its flares.
How come you weren't at the big bash?

How you would like to transcend this primate
sadness (*what bash?*) we try to understand
and salve with poems, paintings, songs, or prayer—

solo protests against solitude — a repertoire
reeling you back beyond years to that amnio
cosmos before chords, major, minor,

diminished: just a slow, enveloping tempo
without tune, before mother
casts you out to face the band.

JUNE CANCELLATION

You make this small deposit to bank away, draw down
maybe years from now, in some sleeping pill season —
how the teens you're coaching, women,
almost, are all relegated to girlhood
by the storm.
          A synaptic charge
arcs the dusk — grand mal in the grey matter
of the clouds — and already the crash
cleaves you. Referee's whistle, first drops
spatting, and the girls are all fleeing,
cleats in hand, teams mixing
amid synchronous laughter,
none knowing now or caring
who won or lost,
          as in the lost
novice seasons, years before this June
of mind-shears and limbic storms, self-
hunger, self-harm, many torrents far less
dodgeable than this storm,
and they will dodge this one,
and they know it,
          hence this riot
of evening reprieve, the school year almost served
and they shoeless on these rain-cool fields,
running — as if there is, while there is — home.

THE WAKING COMES LATE

Year by year the lindens he planted with his mother
tap deeper into the hills, root higher into the winds,
the slender limbs at midwinter stripped, the skies
Frisian blue. And on the lee slope a few hundred
spruce, once seedlings, now fill in
a solid, sun-annulling acre,
though they turn out to be balsam fir, not spruce,
her mistake and his, or maybe his alone —
in those days he assumed all evergreens
were "pines," or "spruce," whatever,
beyond his ego's stunted reach it was all whatever,
all lazy approximation. Now he believes little matters more
than knowing right names.

But the waking comes late.
In the early evening of a life, with dusk
redoubling in a still hectare of hemlock,
tamarack, redcone cedar, you might stir
out of self-induced coma and stare
years down into the mind —

                 too late, you might fear, this insight,
like others before it, might wane, the crucial life-change
fail to hold.
        Out of the spruce swale
he climbs a knoll into a third and final stand
they sowed a few weeks before she died,
during a brief and happy remission,
she looking years younger, quietly pleased
how the steroids had puffed her face enough
to fill in wrinkles, pad out the bones.

In ambering October light they dug
nursling birches into the knoll's bare scalp —
so now with every spring, it too seems
softened, freshened, aging in reverse,
while under the earth the roots of each
in fierce secrecy radiate like veins, fusing
further down into riches,
where all the mothers,
unfinished
unfolding,
remain.

NEW POEMS

CHRISTMAS WORK DETAIL, SAMOS

*Eid milad majid**

In the olive grove on the high ground, facing west
into rain, we dig graves for three men drowned
in the straits — Syrians, maybe, dispossessed
of everything by the sea, so there's no knowing

for sure. This much you can say for any grave,
it's landlocked. And these men will lie a decent
distance uphill, out of sight of the beach
where on Sunday their bodies washed ashore

in plausible orange life-vests (ten Euros each)
packed with sawdust, bubble wrap, rags. These rains
haven't softened the soil, yet digging up here
feels only right; the waves that buried them

terrified them first, and we guess, again,
that they — like the ones the crossing didn't kill —
were from desert towns, the sea inconceivable
as the Arctic. And each cardboard casket,

awaiting its patient passenger, looks
almost seaworthy after the cut-rate raft
they fled in, and which, deflated, washed in
later, silent, as if shyly contrite.

It seems we've failed them, despite the safe graves.
In a grove this untended the ground is brined
bitter with black fruit rotting, and on islands
nowhere is far enough from the waves.

* — Arabic for *Happy birth feast,* or *Merry Christmas*

EASTER ON THE SALISH SEA

Soles cut numb in clamshell shallows.
Turn shoreward: sheer to the zenith,
steeps of old growth are razored
clean to soil, a stubble of umber.

And the last colossus, shorn
to limbless, barkless lumber,
floats like a gangland corpse
face down in shorewater,

shrinking, as dead things do
in Ovidian dreams, as if such mythic
worlds could cease, as if
this were a dream.

FAKE NEWS

An American bodyguard foresees his death

Do I love my country less than I pledged
since I haven't yet brought the tent top down
on this circus? *Head clown*, me and the men

code-call him, in small font, or else imPOTUS —
though so far he seems all too robust. True,
top-story status beats any blood tonic

or drug; the powerful never kick the bucket
without a shove. But if some fanatic
does attempt to off him (snipe him, stab him,

body-bomb him), my Navy SEAL–trained nerves
will trigger a textbook-expert tackle —
not of the perp, you understand, but the Oval

Officer himself. I'll cloak him like a flak
vest of flesh, pin him down behind the podium,
block bullets with my skull, spine, sacrum,

who knows, while gamely the band finishes
"Hail to the Chief" and streamers go on showering
the crowd, their cheers sharpened to screams

as I bleed out, locked in his trembling arms.

AKIN TO A LIZARD

A small desert terrarium contained him
within a larger terrarium, escape meant merely
an exchange of captivities, small wonder
he couldn't swallow. In his see-through throat
the life throbbed slowly, a quasar of plasma,
while beyond that blockage the rest of him
palsied and caved, until he seemed akin
to a hunger artist in a kennel of chaff.

The sunlamp, clearly, he mistook
for a sun; my observing face now and then
eclipsed it; my hand I could, and did, position
to replicate a passing cloud.

But nourishment I never once denied him,
his favourite dainties dispensed
with a lavish hand, mealworms, midges,
succulent crickets who creaked their autumn threnody
before vanishing into his mouth.
                              And what a busy mouth
he had, for a starveling! I repeat, it was rare
that he could swallow past the glowing
bolus of that heart.

Why, in that case, did I push him to try?
My cursive notes and spreadsheets prove
I went on trying, weighing him
(twice daily), forcing him

as if my love and loathing
were fused, gene
to gene,
      please, I repeated,
                eat, eat, eat,
autumn, autumn, autumn.

BETTER THE BLUES (UNPLUGGED)

And suicide, what was that? Surely nothing picturesque or lyrical, like opening
one's veins with a clamshell in a clawfoot tub . . . In the end, seeing it could be
nothing but an aesthetic failure, the aesthete refused.

— Stamátis Smýrlis

Move over, loser
loops the whisper
deep in the larynx
of the solo stumbler,
misstep master, dauntless
squanderer.

Mister needs a fix,
wants a midlife launderer —
late-life coach, downhill doula.
A tactful tape and ruler
to alter the metrics, nudge the data.
Buffer, taller, cooler!

Useless, useless, taunts his pulse
in footnote trochees, though who'd ever guess
by his face or eyes. "He's somebody else
entirely," you'd deduce.
                         Disgrace
so tacit, quiet (as though a ruse,
a hidden facet) no eye
can spy it.

Merrily down, less merrily down the,
less than married now. New
town, seeks single room. Says warily

Onward, wryly, *Nonward*
noneward
unward
doneward.

Loser, so long,
loops the whisper
deep in the larynx
of the solo stumbler.

Still, he figures — or is heard
to mumble — better the blues
than no-song.

PREVÉZA

(Kóstas Karyotákis, 1928)

Death is that mob of jackdaws clattering
over the sombre walls and the shingles,
death, the women who are loved
the same way you scrub an onion.

Death, these squalid, irrelevant streets
with their grand and dazzling titles,
the olive grove, the encircling sea — even
the sun itself, a death among deaths.

Death the cop with his thumb on the scale
weighing out a paltry portion.
Death that hyacinth on the balcony,
the schoolmaster with his daily headlines.

The base, the sentry, the local battalion.
Come Sunday we'll all hear the band.
At the bank, they gave me a savings booklet —
first deposit, thirty drachmas.

You say, walking slowly on the quay,
"Do I exist?" and then, "You don't exist!"
Flag flying, a ship nears. Could be
his honour the governor is arriving.

Out of all these people, if only one
would just drop dead of disgust! Muted,
rueful, with a seemly decorum,
we'd all have fun at the funeral.

190

DREAM FRAGMENT

In those days the weather was jealous
and would turn up at her house just to see
what its cold winds could make of her face.

At her door she would be seen often
speaking to each of the seasons in turn
though with a marked preference
(as many observed, and reported)
for winter

which always stayed longest
and left behind fading signs
of its tenure aboveground.

Who among us up here
wouldn't want his love, her love
to carry a trace that clear, that
cold, stoic and austere, withdrawing
to regain itself, then resurging?

What I wouldn't do
or undo (winter whispered
in a voice akin to mine) to see
one more time what my touch
might make of your face.

NIGHT SKATERS, SKELETON PARK

Puck pummels the boards, a wrister
rings the crossbar, whispers in netting,
razoring strides shave up crystal grit. Plays
unwitnessed score their own applause —
mister, it's like making the finals,
only finer —
                a mosaic, ice-frieze, fresco,
the scratched and cross-hatched drafts of a poem.
Rink lights fade but your blades grind on,
plying tunes from the grooves
like needles do on white-hot vinyl.

FAMILIAL

(Jacques Prévert, 1945)

Mother is knitting a sweater
The son's away at war
It's all good, she thinks, whatever
And the father, what about the father
What's he up to (Business)
The mother with her knitting
The son away at war
And Daddy at his business
It's all good, thinks Dad, whatever
And the son, whatever thinks the son
Sonny thinks exactly nothing
The mother knits the father counts the son fights wars
When the war is over finally
He'll count too in business with his father
The war isn't over and it isn't over
The mother knitting sweaters and sweaters
And Daddy doing his business forever
The son is killed, for him it's all over
Off to the graveyard go mother and father
C'est la vie they figure *c'est la guerre*
Life gets on with its killing its knitting its counting its getting
Its wars its business its sweaters
Business gets on with business, it's business
The filling of orders, the following orders
Life gets on with filling the graveyard

HEAD OF AN OLD MAN WITH CURLY HAIR

(Rembrandt van Rijn, 1659)

He has put away his hands and sealed his lips —
which anyway you can hardly see beneath the rabbinical
beard — as if he no longer needs to gesture or speak,
his gaze speech enough. And it is, even now

with his eyelight dimmed (the source must lie
behind him in the room, a transom or dormer
in midwinter). An old man's window, like his eyes,
ears, mouth, takes in less and less of the world, until

finally none; no sunroof in a sepulchre, no skylight
in a tomb. Yet within this frame, in what photons
persist, his stare arrests, accosts us — not pensive or weary
as we first felt (scrolling past the old, as we do)

but urgent, facetiming us from centuries off,
his patience lessening, shaded eyes demanding:
What are you doing there subtracting yourself
from the light? Or constraining your view

to the blue dormer of a screen you stare into
as if to glimpse a future you've already, frankly,
given away. You the self-unseen, you the self-
eclipsed. If it's not your screen, it's your mirror. I

hold my breath for you all. It pains me to watch, even
this far removed. Your young are worst off, clearly,
though for them I still feel hope; it's not so hard to be happy,
billions have managed before you, and with far less.

I've managed. True, my day is mostly spent, and
here too there's no reckoning the lonely, the broken.
But my world is dirty, poor, and dim. What could be the reason
in your case? Staring at shadows!

My judgement may seem hasty, my tenor rude,
but the eleventh hour is every hour, as any old man
can vouch. I stand by every word, though I've spoken
none aloud. (He has sealed his lips, put away his hands,

and now his eyes, too, conclude.)

LISTEN . . .

(Gottfried Benn, 1955)

. . . here is how your final evening will pass
when you're still capable of going out.
At the café door you'll smoke your Players
or sit at a small table with your glass —
a house bitter, Scotch, then your usual stout —

reading news of shattered ceasefires on your phone.
Did I mention you're alone,
closed off, unless you count the radiator,
its undemanding warmth? Around you humans
blatting, that pair with their drooling Weimaraner.

You're no more than this. No house to your name,
no hill or high window from which to dream
over a sprawling sunscape. You've always shut
the walls tightly around you, from your birth
until tonight . . . You were no more than this, sure,

yet Zeus and the pantheon, the universe,
the great souls, all the suns were there for you too,
surging through you in streams — you were this
and no more, now finished as begun,
your final evening out — sweet dreams.

SHIP'S PILOT NAGEL

(*Níkos Kavvadías, 1933*)

Nagel Harvor, Norwegian pilot at Colombo,
after carefully guiding past the breakwater
ships headed for ports remote and unknown,
would hunker in the pilothouse, pensive, sober,
his heavy arms folded across his chest,
smoking an old clay pipe and muttering to himself
in his northern tongue. He would head back to port
once the ships had vanished.

He'd been a cargo vessel captain until, one day,
having sailed and seen the world, he grew weary
and stayed on as a pilot in Colombo.
But he was always thinking of his far-off home
in the Lofotens, that storied archipelago,
and one day at the wheel silently he died
after guiding out the tanker *Fjord Folden*
as she steamed away for the Lofoten Islands.

DAWN, AFTER THE SPRING SUICIDES

At dawn each day the gods
pour more thought into this world, light,
colour, contour, dimension

returning. But for some neighbours,
their crises quietly evolving
a wall or two away,

there comes no clear waking,
no threshold thaw; the dark
of course undeniably

was dark, but at the same time
had the decency to disguise the world
and lend hope that dawn (if it deigned

to upload) might display a planet
refreshed, reframed —
no hinterlife, no eunuch

twilight, the fast unbroken and panic
by the plateful: a lone vet
loading his gun and unloading;

the pregnant one who stockpiles percs,
30 small white pillows
for a month of sleeps . . .

Each day at dawn the gods
pour more thought into this world, light,
colour, contour deepening by degrees,

the sun steepening on the causeway
and the willows like green-gowned
brides, while discreetly

the neighbouring shades recede,
the world punching in for
its dayshift amnesia.

SINGING IN THE GRAVE

In the dream, the brother I do not have
says something about singing in the grave.
I understand him to mean *singing*
in the graveyard but don't correct him —
I'm astonished that he exists at all,
though I may in fact have had a brother, briefly,
who can say; when I was a child, folks rarely
spoke of the ones who arrived months too soon
or else on time but stubbornly
holding their breath forever.

When our boy was stillborn
I held him up to the sun crowning
from the lake ten storeys below the ward window
and the molten light made his eyes alive.
At times I hate the word *seem*
so I just say *alive* though I do not sing it
in the way my brother's spirit-double
now seems to urge.

While I had the chance I should have asked him
(brother, son), Why is it when you half-wake
from the high cirrus of sleep
to dreamed music, it's already fading,
gone, it can never be remembered
or set down?

Like mine and my brother's,
his eyes were dark brown.

MIDNIGHT VARIATIONS

1
In the wall by my ear
as I sit writing
a bat scratches.

2
We renew our midnight
treaty — I at my desk
and she in the wall
signifying something.

3
I'm fine with this truce —
she minding her side
of the fence, I
minding mine.

4
By my ear, in the hibernaculum
I choose to humour, a bat stirs,
rustling, chittering
as they always do
when a midwinter thaw
revives them.
          One creature
famished, foraging in its cell,
one willing a blank page
to yield words.

Stalin's Carnival

In the summer of 1986 I happened on a brick-thick paperback of Robert Payne's magisterial *The Rise and Fall of Stalin*. While tearing through it I discovered that Stalin, when young, had been an idealistic, romantic poet of some promise. Fascinated, disturbed, I started handwriting a manic first draft of a coming-of-age novel about Stalin's (Josef Djugashvili's) youth. Needless to say, I had no idea what I was doing. The manuscript included my free approximations of several of the young Stalin's published poems, along with many invented poems — the ones he might conceivably have written had he continued to write poetry. (Those approximations first whetted my appetite for translation, a practice that has become central to my writing.) In the end, nothing of that three-hundred-page draft survived except one approximation and a few of the invented poems. They, along with others that I wrote in '87 and '88 to complete the sequence, became "Ashes on the Earth: Selected Works of Josef Stalin" — the centrepiece of my first book, *Stalin's Carnival*. I remain grateful to Robert Hilderley, of Quarry Press, for reading that hastily handwritten manuscript — think about that — and encouraging me to extricate the poems and build on them instead.

Foreign Ghosts

In 2006, Dawn Marie Kresan, under her Palimpsest Press imprint, handmade eighty copies of a chapbook called *Paper Lanterns: 25 Postcards from Asia*. Along with photographs by Mary Huggard, it contained poems and journal entries selected from *Foreign Ghosts*, a full-length book in the Japanese *utaniki* (song-diary) form, published by Oberon Press in 1990 but long out of print. The versions of the *Foreign Ghosts* poems that appear in this volume are taken from that chapbook.

The Ecstasy of Skeptics

Both "Elegy as a Message Left on an Answering Machine" and "Glosa" were written in memory of my friend, the writer and teacher Tom Marshall (1938–1993).

"In Heraclitus's City": The ruins depicted in the poem are those of the ancient Greek city of Ephesus, founded some three millennia ago on the Aegean coast of Asia Minor, in what is now Turkey's Izmir province.

The third section of "Takayama" is after a poem by a Japanese poet of the Heian period, Ono no Komachi.

The Address Book

The American Night Listens": The reference in line 10 is to actor Jack MacGowran's great reading of Beckett's fiction on the Claddagh LP *MacGowran Speaking Beckett*. The poem's first two lines are from a dream.

"The Last Speaker of the Arondha Tongue . . ." is for David O'Meara.

"Lost Waterfalls." Some years ago, the Kingston poet Eric Folsom, while doing research on the Cataraqui River and its tributaries for his book *Poems for Little Cataraqui* (Broken Jaw Press, 1998), found a two-century-old reference to a waterfall north of Kingston, east of the Perth Road. I owe "Lost Waterfalls" to Folsom's research and his poem cycle.

Patient Frame

"You Know Who You Are": John Austen Gallienne, formerly the choirmaster at St. George's Cathedral, Kingston. May his many victims, dead and alive, find peace.

"Some Other Just Ones": The poem's italicized first and last lines are translated from Jorge Luis Borges's poem "Los justos" ("The Just").

Stamátis Smýrlis is the *nom de plume* of the Greek poet Strátis Apanópolis (1939–).

The Waking Comes Late

"The City" is one of the best-known poems of Cavafy (Konstantínos Kaváfis), and a number of literally accurate English translations exist. But even the best one of these, by Edmund Keeley and Philip Sherrard, is more a rendering in prose — albeit fluent, elegant prose — than a poetic translation. In my opinion, a translator should try to represent not only the content of the original but also its form and sound, especially if the poem has a rhyme scheme, as does "The City."

Since the poem is written in such straightforward, transparent Greek, there can be little argument among translators about how to render particular word choices or metaphorical constructions. Hence readers will find little difference between the various unrhymed English versions of the poem. What most of these versions do convey well is the stately, processional movement of Cavafy's thoughts and words — and without question this movement is a key part of Cavafy's poetic signature. But in "The City," the other vital component is rhyme.

Of course, translators who do attempt to re-enact the verbal music of a poem like "The City" may fail in their own ways. In trying to approximate the effect of Cavafy's end-rhymed Greek, I've used consonantal — and, in one or two cases, assonantal — rhyme, for the usual reason: English is a relatively rhyme-poor tongue, and the consonantal system evens the field for English-language translators, allowing them to achieve the effect of rhyme without overly distorting and deforming the poem's movement. A liberal use of internal rhyme, I feel, helps support and deepen the effect. [Postscript, October 2020: the poet and scholar Evan Jones has just published, with Carcanet, a comprehensive and very good translation of much of Cavafy's poetry and prose: *The Barbarians Arrive Today*. Jones's version of "The City" likewise tries to approximate the poem's essential form, and with great success.]

"Coronach, Post-Kandahar" is in memory of — though not about — CFB Kingston storesman Patrick Martin Kelly (1954–2014)

"The Weather Online" is a kind of approximation of Lucinda Williams's song "I Envy the Wind" (from her 2001 album, *Essence*). Williams's beautiful song is itself a kind of approximation of Emily Dickinson's poem 498, "I envy seas, whereon he rides."

New poems

"Head of an Old Man with Curly Hair" — a response to a 1659 Rembrandt van Rijn painting in the Agnes Etherington Art Centre, Kingston, Ontario — was commissioned in 2019 by Andrea Gunn, editor of the *Queen's Alumni Review*, and Jan Allen, the gallery's retired director.

"Night Skaters, Skeleton Park" was commissioned by Greg Tilson and the Skeleton Park Arts Festival. The poem was inscribed on the boards of the park's skating rink in the winter of 2018.

"Listen . . .", an approximation of Gottfried Benn's "Hör zu," I undertook at the urging of Richard Sanger, who was creating his own version of the poem. So this translation is for him.

Sophie Mayer read an early draft of "Midnight Variations" and told me that I seemed to be rewriting, in a highly compressed form, the 9th-century Old Irish poem "Pangur Bán," a work that to my embarrassment I had never heard of, let alone read.

ACKNOWLEDGEMENTS: MAGAZINES & ANTHOLOGIES

I've tried to list here the publications in which my poems have appeared over the years. I'm grateful to each and every editor — but especially so to the first few who accepted and published my work.

Magazines

Agni, Anthos, Antigonish Review, Arc, Ariel, Books in Canada, Brick, Canadian Literature, Carousel, Crash, Dalhousie Review, Dandelion, Descant, Dusie, Eighteen Bridges, Estuaire, Event, Exile, The Fiddlehead, Geist, The Globe & Mail, Grain, Grind, The Irish Examiner, Kansas Quarterly, Lichen, Lines Review, The Literary Review, London Magazine, London Review of Books, The Malahat Review, Matrix, Moosehead Review, The Moth, The New Canadian Review, The New Quarterly, Next Exit, Oversion, Poem, Poetry Australia, Poetry Canada Review, Poetry (Chicago), Poetry London, PRISM International, Proserpine Press, Prospice, Quadrant, Quarry, Queen's Alumni Review, Queen's Quarterly, Queen Street Quarterly, Revue Europe (French translations by Judith Cowan), *The Rialto, Scrivener, subTERRAIN, Taproot, University of Windsor Review, Wascana Review, The Walrus, Waves, Writers' Forum, Zymergy*

"Some Other Just Ones" was broadcast on the BBC radio program *Something Understood* and on the BBC World Service, April 2009.

Anthologies

The Best American Poetry, 2012 (Scribner, ed. Mark Doty)
The Best Canadian Poetry, 2009 (Tightrope Books, ed. A. F. Moritz)
The Best Canadian Poetry, 2011 (Tightrope, ed. Priscila Uppal)
The Best Canadian Poetry, 2016 (Tightrope, ed. Helen Humphreys)

The Best of Walrus Poetry (Walrus eBooks, ed. Michael Lista)

The Exile Book of Poems in Translation (Exile Editions, ed. Priscila Uppal)

15 Canadian Poets × 3 (Oxford University Press, ed. Gary Geddes)

The New Canon (Signal Editions, ed. Carmine Starnino)

Modern Canadian Poets (Carcanet, ed. Evan Jones & Todd Swift)

Poets '88 (Quarry Press, ed. by Bob Hilderley & Ken Norris)

Québec Suite (Muses Company, ed. Endre Farkas)

Richard Outram: Essays on His Work (Guernica, ed. Ingrid Ruthig)

Scapes (ed. Diane Dawber)

71 (+) for George Bowering (Coach House Books, ed. Jean Baird, David McFadden, George Stanley)

The Sea: A Literary Companion (Greystone Books, ed. Wayne Grady)

Telling Stories, Secret Lives (Agnes Etherington Art Centre, ed. Jan Allen)

Thru the Smoky End Boards (Polestar Press, ed. Kevin Brooks & Sean Brooks)

Vintage '91 (Sono Nis Press)

Written in the Skin (Insomniac Press, ed. rob mclennan)

What the Poets Are Doing (Nightwood Editions, ed. Rob Taylor)

Refugium: Poems of the Pacific (Caitlin Press, ed. Yvonne Blomer)

Sweet Water: Poems for the Watersheds (Caitlin Press, ed. Yvonne Blomer)

Jailbreaks: 99 Canadian Sonnets (Biblioasis, ed. Zachariah Wells)

Kingston Poets' Gallery (Artful Codger Press, ed. Elizabeth Greene)

Written in Stone (Quarry Press, ed. Bob Hilderley)

The Yalova Festival Anthology (ed. Lale Müldür)

Ledger of Thanks

First, the editors of the individual collections, in chronological order: Robert Hilderley; Dilshad Engineer; Michael Redhill & Don McKay; Ken Babstock & Don McKay; Ken Babstock; Damian Rogers; and, for this selected volume, Karen Solie.

Wanting to give credit and gratitude where they're due, I tried amalgamating the six personal acknowledgements lists from the individual collections. Far too long. In the end, I've focused on those family members and colleagues whose contribution was especially large and concrete. I've shortened the list further by not repeating the names of people cited above or among the magazine and anthology acknowledgements, nor the names of those to whom I've dedicated poems. And I've tried to list names in loose chronological order, a kind of personal history of influence, guidance, and support.

John Heighton, Mary Huggard, Leslie Monkman, Edward Lobb, Victor Coleman, Mark Sinnett, Tom Marshall, David Helwig, Al and Eurithe Purdy, David Manicom, Joanne Page, Kim Jernigan, Richard Lemm, Brian Bartlett, Michael Holmes, Jay Ruzesky, Michael Redhill, Don Coles, Karen Connelly, Mary Cameron, Judith Cowan, Brian Brett, Ingrid Ruthig, Peter duChemin, Jenny Haysom, Martha Sharpe, Elena Heighton, Alexander Scala, Heather Frise, Nyla Matuk, Amanda Jernigan/Luke Hathaway, Michael Harris, Shane Neilson, Sandra Ridley, Alvin Lee, Kevin Connolly, Maria Golikova, and Ginger Pharand.

Finally, my thanks to the Ontario Arts Council and the Canada Council for their support of these poems and my publishers over the years.

S.H., Kingston, October 2020

STEVEN HEIGHTON's poetry collections include *The Waking Comes Late,* which received the 2016 Governor General's Award; *Stalin's Carnival,* winner of the 1990 Gerald Lampert Award; *The Ecstasy of Skeptics,* a 1995 Governor General's Award finalist; *The Address Book,* poems from which received the Petra Kenney Prize and a gold National Magazine Award; and *Patient Frame,* poems from which received the P. K. Page Award and a silver National Magazine Award. Heighton is also the author of several acclaimed works of fiction and nonfiction, including the 2020 Hilary Weston Prize finalist *Reaching Mithymna: Among the Volunteers and Refugees on Lesvos* and the novel *Afterlands,* a *New York Times Book Review* Editors' Choice and a best of year selection in ten publications in Canada, the U.S., and the U.K. His poems and stories have appeared in *Granta, London Review of Books, Poetry, Tin House, Zoetrope, Best American Poetry, The Walrus, TLR, Agni, New England Review, Brick, Best Canadian Poetry,* and *Best English Stories.* He lives in Kingston, Ontario.

In 2021, Wolfe Island Records will release an album of his songs, *The Devil's Share.* To listen, visit www.wolfeislandrecords.com/stevenheighton.